AVALANCHE

ALSO BY MELINDA BRAUN

Stranded

AVALANCHE

MELINDA BRAUN

SIMON PULSE
New York London Toronto Sydney New Delhi

SIMON PULSE

An imprint of Simon & Schuster Children's Publishing Division

1230 Avenue of the Americas, New York, New York 10020

First Simon Pulse paperback edition November 2017

Text copyright © 2016 by Simon & Schuster, Inc.

Cover photographs copyright © 2016 by

Tim Daniels/Arcangel Images (landscape); Soren Egeberg/Offset.com (skiers)

Also available in a Simon Pulse hardcover edition.

For information about special discounts for bulk purchases, please contact

Simon & Schuster Special Sales at 1-866-506-1949 or business@simonandschuster.com.

The Simon & Schuster Speakers Bureau can bring authors to your live event.

For more information or to book an event contact the Simon & Schuster Speakers Bureau at 1-866-248-3049 or visit our website at www.simonspeakers.com.

Book designed by Steve Scott

The text of this book was set in Absara.

Manufactured in the United States of America

2   4   6   8   10   9   7   5   3   1

The Library of Congress has cataloged the hardcover edition as follows:

Names: Braun, Melinda, author. Title: Avalanche / by Melinda Braun.

Description: Simon Pulse hardcover edition. | New York : Simon Pulse, 2016. |

Summary: "After an avalanche hits, a group of skiers in the Rocky Mountains must survive Mother Nature and a life-threatening injury to one of their members in order to make it out of the mountains and find help"—Provided by publisher.

Identifiers: LCCN 2016015853| ISBN 9781481438223 (hc) | ISBN 9781481438247 (eBook)

Subjects: | CYAC: Survival—Fiction. | Avalanches—Fiction. | BISAC: JUVENILE FICTION / Action & Adventure / Survival Stories. | JUVENILE FICTION / Social Issues / Physical & Emotional Abuse (see also Social Issues / Sexual Abuse). | JUVENILE FICTION / Social Issues / New Experience.

Classification: LCC PZ7.B737785 Av 2016 | DDC [Fic]—dc23

LC record available at https://lccn.loc.gov/2016015853

ISBN 9781481438230 (pbk)

For my brother and sister,

Jimmy and Kelly

DAY 4

MATT
Location: Unknown

He stood motionless in the swirling snowfall, the dead branch balanced lightly over his shoulder like a gnarled baseball bat. He stared at the trees for movement. Past dusty green spruces and giant blue-needled firs, between slim aspens and their black spiderlike branch tips swollen and ready to bud. Though the forest was silent, he knew it was there. And he knew it was watching. But they couldn't run.

Not anymore.

So Matt waited. Ignoring the throb pulsing through his ruined feet, he wished for the hundredth time that he was somewhere else—anywhere else. Despite all the things that had happened in the past three days, or maybe because of them, Matt refused to accept that he would die here. Not now. Not like this. Not after everything they'd gone through. Then again, he figured there must be a limit to luck—it had to run out eventually. This was just as good a time as any. Just as good a place. Out here, death came easy.

But he wasn't going to die without a fight.

The snow fell faster; thick, feathery flakes obliterated the landscape around him into a downy blur of white. The trees disappeared; the mountains beyond them vanished. No birdcalls, no wind, no sound at all except his own breath. Matt's thoughts drifted to memories of youthful violence, and he wondered if it was because of what was about to happen. Because of what he was going to need to do. *Fight.* He wondered if he remembered how.

Third grade was the first and last time he'd ever been in a fight. A real one, with punches and kicks and bruised stomachs. And now, hungry as he was, Matt easily recalled the taste of dirty knuckles colliding with his teeth, the sensation of biting down into skin. But he couldn't remember the reason—*why* the fight had happened. He did, however, remember the who.

Dennis Greene. *Mean, mean Denny Greene. The biggest jerk you've ever seen.* Matt and Dennis hadn't liked each other on sight. And it didn't take long for Dennis—in all his eight-year-old glorious psychopathy—to walk up to Matt and say, "At recess, I'm gonna kick your ass," punching his fist into his palm. *Smack. Smack. Smack.* Matt didn't understand why he was given a warning, unless it was just a form of psychological torture, which turned out to be an effective tactic.

When recess arrived Dennis chased him, picked Matt off from the pack like a lion attacking a weakened gazelle, herded him against a brick wall. And like a hive of bees the rest of the students swarmed in for a better look.

Moments later, Matt and Dennis marched down the long, shiny hallway to the principal's office. Dennis went in first, coming out only a few minutes later, his head down in shame or embarrassment—Matt couldn't be sure.

What he was sure of was that the principal had been surprised to see him. Matt wasn't a known troublemaker, wasn't the type to get into a fight. But these weren't really the reasons why the principal stared so bewilderedly at Matt. It was because Dennis Greene *looked* like he'd been hit by a bus. Swollen eye, puffy lips, a missing tooth, and a bright pink bite mark on his forearm, almost breaking the skin. And Matt—Matt who at age eight had the same build as a fence post—didn't have a mark on him, only a T-shirt slightly stretched out around the collar.

"I want to hear your story," the principal finally said, folding his arms over his chest as he leaned back against his desk, the wood creaking under his weight.

But there wasn't a story to tell. Matt just shrugged and mumbled his way through an explanation. The principal sighed, and dismissed him back to class, saying, "You're pretty lucky, you know. And you're a good kid."

But the principal had been wrong. Matt wasn't a good kid; he just looked like one. Because during the fight, after Dennis landed his first punch in Matt's stomach, Matt twisted into Dennis and thought two things.

Did he really just punch me in the guts? (The radiating

heat through his lower intestines told him the answer was a definite yes.)

I'm going to kill you, Dennis Greene.

They stared, eye-to-eye, before Matt erupted with a sound that was half cat hiss and half screech owl. "I'm gonna eat you alive!" He sunk his teeth deep into Dennis's forearm, followed by a furious windmilling of his fists, rapid jabs to Dennis's face until he was cowering on the ground, bloodied and breathless.

Dennis never bothered Matt again. Not because he'd earned the bully's respect—not by a long shot. But because Dennis saw something in Matt's eyes that day, something he knew to avoid. A type of deep primal fear that triggered an automatic recoil, like walking into a giant spiderweb.

A flash of gold caught Matt's eyes, dragging him back to the present. Here, in this wildness, he no longer needed luck. What he needed was to become that kid again—the raging third grader he thought he'd left behind.

William Faulkner was right, he thought. *The past is never dead. It's not even past.*

Matt clutched the broken tree branch and watched the animal slink into the pines, moving through the whiteout like a ghost.

He gave the branch a quick squeeze, testing his grip, and exhaled small puffs of steam as he waited. And waited . . .

And waited.

DAY 1

MATT
*Location: **Somewhere over Nebraska***
*Elevation: **36,000 feet***

Matt Ruban, all six feet and one hundred ninety-two pounds of him, squirmed in his seat as he passed an unused barf bag to his best friend, Tony. Matt pressed the flight attendant call button, but the light didn't work. *Great.* This made him anxious, even more anxious than being trapped next to someone emptying their guts into a paper sack, so he jabbed at it three more times. Staring down the length of the aisle for someone in uniform, he tried to ignore another disturbing thought. *If the attendant button doesn't work on this plane, what else doesn't work?*

Matt, fully conscious of the seat's metal frame pressing against his hips, began to wonder about the size and shape of things, especially airplane compartments. Everything seemed to have been designed to accommodate much smaller humans, kids really. Even though at seventeen Matt was technically still considered a kid, there was nothing juvenile about his stature or appearance. Except for his face, which was still smooth-skinned and absent of the acne that plagued most teenage boys. Matt looked older than seventeen, he knew, and he ruffled his short, dark brown hair—too long to be described as military— and scratched at the stubble of sideburns that refused to extend past the tips of his ears. His eyes were as dark as a rainstorm, and his thin lips were pinched in embarrassment for himself and concern for his friend. The engine drone of the Airbus A320 was almost enough to drown out the sound of Tony's retching. Almost.

Matt leaned over his armrest into the aisle. The plane was half empty, which gave the impression of more space, but at the same time there was a sense of organized tightness around him, a geometrical precision of compartments and square outlines and corners that prevented him from getting comfortable. Matt squirmed back into his seat as Tony gave another heave into the bag, and he took that as yet another sign he should never have agreed to this trip. *That's what? Sign number five?* Matt had been keeping track since morning.

In fact, he even had a list. Like an *actual* list. On a piece of paper, crunched up in his back pocket.

Number one: The flight being delayed due to fog on the ground in Des Moines.

Number two: The flight being delayed again for "mechanical reasons." Reasons which were never explained. Reasons Matt didn't want to know about.

Number three: Tony deciding to order shrimp cocktail in the airport restaurant while they waited.

Number four: A drunk guy who was not allowed to board the flight (due to his drunkenness), who then began to verbally abuse the gate agent. "Don't you know who the hell I am?" he screamed into her face.

She didn't.

Neither did anyone else, apparently. So, in a fit of rage, Mr. Drunk Businessman ripped his boarding pass in half, tripped on his own wheelie bag, and landed against a large potted palm tree that smashed to the floor, spilling dirt everywhere.

Remembering the list, Matt knew this whole trip was a mistake. Technically, he wasn't supposed to be here, not on a plane heading west. He was supposed to be flying to Florida with his father for spring break. "It'll be great," his father said. "A warm and sunny week full of baseball and beaches and fishing on Marco Island!" But the plans fell through, as they always seemed to when his father was involved. A work problem. A schedule problem. A girl-friend problem.

His father called him on the phone a month ago to cancel, filling the conversation with hasty apologies and immediate assurances to reschedule. Matt almost bought it, too, until his dad told him the real news. Why he really needed to cancel. Why his new wife's needs were suddenly more important. And that made Matt say things he'd thought many times before but never spoke aloud, including the last sentence before hanging up.

"You're fifty-three years old and you're still a god-damned idiot!"

Matt squeezed his fist around the end of the armrest. Though he hadn't done anything but sit in his seat for the past hour, his heart was pounding, his throat dry and itchy at the memory. That he hated feeling this way was an understatement, and he gave the armrest one more squeeze as the flight attendant stopped next to him. The button must have worked after all.

"Can I help—oh . . . ," she began, before glancing over at Tony slumped in his seat.

"Yes. Sorry," Matt said, the only explanation he could manage as he handed over the putrid sack. "Sorry," he repeated. If the flight attendant was repulsed, she didn't show it, but kept smiling, as if the swollen bag was a Christmas present. Matt guessed she'd seen a lot worse.

"Should I bring another?" she chirped.

"Umm, yeah. Thanks." She's pretty, Matt realized, in a carefully made-up way. Too much makeup, though. "Some ginger ale would be good?" It came out sounding like a question.

"Of course. One ginger ale."

"Make it two," Matt said. "Please." He was suddenly hungry. Starving. Despite having to listen to Tony's stomach exercises. "Do you have any pretzels? Nuts?"

"I'll check. We do have a selection of lunch items for purchase."

"No thanks." Matt shook his head. If he could eat

free he would. Besides, he knew they'd eat when they landed. *Forty-five minutes,* Matt reasoned. He could certainly wait that long. A year ago he would have paid for the overpriced snack box. "Just some pretzels if you have any." Perhaps he was making progress.

"Certainly." She blinked her thickly mascaraed eyelashes, which reminded Matt of some sort of insect. "Ginger ale and pretzels."

"Cans of ginger ale," Matt quickly added, shifting again in his seat. "Two cans."

Matt knew if he didn't say that she would bring back two plastic cups, barely full. Nickel and diming everywhere, as his dad would say. Extra for headphones. Extra for peanuts. Pretty soon we'll all have to fly stark naked and be able to fit in the overhead bin because they'll charge extra for the actual seat. Matt bit down on his lip to remove his dad's words from his head. *Florida,* he couldn't help but think. *I was supposed to be going to Florida.*

The flight attendant nodded with a smile that either meant she liked Matt or wanted to punch him in the face—it was impossible to tell, and Matt wondered if they taught that trick in flight attendant school, if there was such a thing. There probably used to be.

"Two cans of ginger ale coming up." She glided away down the aisle.

"Sorry, bro," Tony said.

Matt watched the flight attendant's legs swish away,

a much better view than anything else at the moment. He didn't answer.

"Dude, I am." Tony poked his shoulder. "Totally. I mean it, Matt."

"I know." *Don't call me dude*, Matt thought. For whatever reason, Tony spoke as though he grew up in the San Fernando Valley. In the eighties. When in reality, he grew up in a four-bedroom colonial, beige siding with black shutters, in West Des Moines, Iowa. Tony's place stood two houses down from Matt's, whose own house looked exactly the same, except with navy-blue shutters. They'd known each other since kindergarten.

"I shouldn't have eaten that shrimp," Tony said, somewhat regretfully.

"No kidding."

"I guess I didn't think I'd be eating much for the next week." Tony leaned his head back against the window.

"Your brother knows how to cook," Matt said. "He'll feed us, you know."

"Yeah, dude, but what?"

"Food, I guess. Don't all college students have endless supplies of ramen? They also have this weird thing called restaurants." The flight attendant was on her way back, palming two metallic-green cans. "Besides, this was your idea, remember?"

Tony grunted.

Matt took the cans. "Thank you." They were warm, of course, but he didn't care. He quickly popped the top of one with a satisfying *chaclunk-fwiiisssh*, which never failed to make him thirsty.

Tony slugged his down, drinking half before commenting the obvious. "It's warm."

"You're welcome."

"Sorry. Thanks bro." He smiled and Matt forgave him immediately.

Completely oblivious most of the time, but genuinely nice, Tony reminded Matt of a golden retriever. Self-involved, a little dumb, oafish and gluttonous, but not mean. Never mean. And that was saying something.

"How much longer?" Tony asked, keeping the can pressed to his forehead.

"Not much." Matt poked the button on the headrest screen to pull up the map. The plane icon blinked, a red arrow denoting the flight path. "It looks like we're almost ready to descend."

"Thank God."

"Have patience," Matt replied. "All things are difficult before they become easy."

Tony rolled his eyes. "All right, I'll bite. Tell me who said that one. And it better not be Confucius."

"Saadi."

"Who the heck is that?"

"Persian poet. Lived during the thirteenth century, I think."

"Well, here's what I think." Tony replied, stifling a belch. "I think I don't like flying."

"Nobody *likes* flying," Matt said. "But it's not that bad."

Tony crossed his eyes. "That's because you didn't just empty your lunch into a paper bag."

"Too true." Matt finally smiled.

"Not funny, dude."

"It's a little funny."

"And now I'm hungry again." Tony sighed and drank the rest of his ginger ale.

"Hello and good afternoon. This is your captain. We have begun our descent . . ."

"What's he saying?" Tony whispered nervously.

"It's in English, Tony."

"Oh?" He frowned, unconvinced. "I don't understand it. Must be the accent."

"It's the usual," Matt said. "Weather's good. Sixty-five and sunny." Tony smiled wide at this, considering back in Des Moines it was barely above freezing. "And everything looks good for landing. No delays. We should be on the ground in twenty minutes." Out the window there was nothing but clouds, but soon enough the plane lowered into them. The engine shuddered slightly—a trembling vibration rippled through the cabin, giving everything made of plastic a twisty squeak.

"What's that?" Tony tightened his belt. "Thought you said it's good."

"Just some turbulence coming down over the mountains," Matt lied, having no idea what it was, only that he didn't want Tony to get so nervous that he barfed again. "Perfectly normal."

"How can they land in this?" Tony examined the white fog out the window. "You can't see a thing."

"They don't have to see," Matt explained. "They just use computers. They can do it blindfolded. The plane practically lands itself."

"Says you," Tony fidgeted with the shade on the window. "So what happens when the computers don't work?"

"I guess we crash."

"Dude!" Tony flinched. "Bad juju."

"Sorry."

The plane descended, making Matt's ears pop. He drank the rest of the ginger ale in breathless gulps.

The ground, now visible through the clouds, reminded him of a desert, brown and flat, but north of the downtown buildings the mountains reared up, slate blue, black, and green, bright white on the peaks. *A lot of snow*, Matt thought, dejected. More than he expected for April. Even from this height the mountain range looked immense, dwarfing the city below. He didn't want snow. He wanted sand and palm trees. Hot sun and ocean breezes.

Wing flaps rose in a mechanical whir. Wheels unfolded from the belly, and with a squeak and a judder, the plane touched down.

Matt felt the air decompress and heard the buttons ding. Seat belts unclicked as the captain announced their arrival. "On behalf of the flight crew we wish you a safe and pleasant journey. . . ."

"Are you sure that's English?" Tony interrupted. "I still can't understand a word."

"He says welcome to Denver." Matt tugged his duffle bag free from the overhead bin. "The mile-high city."

"High is right." Tony laughed, pretending to smoke a joint. "Rocky Mountain high, Colorado," he sang, then punched Matt in the shoulder. "Dude! This is going to be the best spring break ever."

Please stop calling me dude. Matt squeezed his eyes shut, pushing away all thoughts of his dad and Florida, determined to acquire the same enthusiasm as his friend. *Fake it till you make it,* he thought. He didn't know who said that, only that it was one of those anonymous quotes everyone uses sooner or later. "You're right." He forced a smile at Tony. "This is gonna be great."

MATT
Location: En route to Boulder, Colorado

The VW bus had seen better days, and all of them happened fifty years ago. Matt figured it was probably built in the late sixties or early seventies. Painted a color somewhere between pea and slime green, its white fenders marbled with rust. The windows were dark and greasy looking; visible fumes belched from the tailpipe, smelling like a combination of sulfur, gasoline, and candy corn. A scent overly sweet and chemical.

"Yo!" Sid climbed out and waved, and Matt couldn't decide what was more surprising: that Sid had been driving the contraption, or that Matt barely recognized him. As Tony's older brother, Sid was slightly taller, sturdier, and now, exponentially better looking than his younger sibling. Tony stood hunched over on the curb, looking somewhat hungover, backpack slung over one shoulder while staring cross-eyed at the bus. He didn't answer or even acknowledge his older brother's presence, but wrinkled his nose and squinted in confusion.

"Let's go, TB!"

TB. Tony's middle name was Bennett. Tony Bennett, just like the singer. His full name was Anthony Bennett Jain, but everyone in his family always called him Tony Bennett. So did everyone in school, up until junior high when he decided to give himself a new nickname, demanding on the first day of seventh grade that everyone must call him TB, not knowing it was the abbreviation for tuberculosis. When he realized his mistake it was too late, which in a way, was sort of like coming down with actual TB.

"What is *that*?" Tony blurted. "The mystery machine? Do you drive around solving crimes?"

Sid grinned, striding forward. "You making fun of me?"

Tony was, of course. "Does Dad know you bought that hippie pile of crap?"

Matt laughed, thinking of Mr. Jain—*Dr.* Jain, actually. Professor of economics at Drake. Watcher of football, DIYer of all things home improvement, ultimate tomato gardener, and in many ways the father Matt never had, even before his own took off when he was twelve. "He would definitely say that purchase is a liability, not even considered a depreciating asset," Matt said, crossing his arms.

"Yeah, but it's not mine. My roommate Carter let me borrow his van to come and pick you douche bags up," Sid replied. "Good to see you, Matt. You putting on weight?" The way Sid said it almost made it into a compliment, and he made a quick jab forward like he was going to punch Matt in the gut. Matt knew this fake out and didn't flinch. He had actually lost ten pounds since he'd last seen Sid, his lowest weight in years, but the tops of his ears burned regardless.

"Losing it." Matt scooped up his duffel. "Now a whopping one hundred and ninety pounds." Sid had always given him crap about his weight. Fatty Matty, Sid called him. Or Fat Boy, Chubba, Pork Belly, Butterball, Tubs, Moonpie, or anything else that Sid happened to think of. Matt had actually been thin as a child, only putting on weight when he hit double digits, arriving at the "clinically obese" mark by thirteen. But then he began to grow (vertically), took up basketball, and stopped eating entire boxes of Little Debbie Swiss Rolls and bags of potato chips in one sitting.

Matt climbed into the van, noting the interior smelled worse than the outside. Dirty vinyl, patchouli and pot, rotten potatoes, and something else he couldn't quite describe. *Old baby diaper?*

Tony jumped in the front. "Dude! It smells like ass in here!"

Sid started the car—surprisingly turning it over without a stutter, engine humming confidently. "That's because you're in it, TB."

"Whatever," Tony grunted. "Someone needs to do some serious Febrezing in here."

The VW cruised out of the airport terminal, merging

on Peña Boulevard to Highway 470, and north to Boulder. "So what's the plan, Sid?" *Tony was right about the Febreze*, Matt thought, the beginnings of nausea creeping in with each breath. He rolled down the window and a dull roar of fresh air filled the bus.

"That is." Sid pointed over the dashboard to the distant mountain range. From this distance the mountains appeared fake, shining snowcapped peaks, like a movie prop instead of the real thing. "That's the plan."

"So what resort?" Tony asked. "Breckenridge? Keystone? Snowmass?"

"Nope."

"What do you mean, *nope*? Where are we going, then?"

"We're not going to a resort. We're gonna do some AT."

"Come again?"

"Alpine touring," Sid said. "The real deal. Serious back country skiing."

"Okay," Matt said, realizing that even though they'd gone at least ten miles the mountains didn't look any closer. "But what's that, exactly?"

"You'll love it." Sid smiled knowingly in the rearview mirror, his teeth perfect white squares. "Don't worry. It's something you're never gonna forget."

Over steaming plates piled with chicken korma, lamb rogan josh, and shrimp biryani, Sid laid out the spring break itinerary. "So you guys, you know how to downhill, right?"

"Of course," Tony said and Matt nodded, taking a bite of shrimp. It was spicy—not scary hot, but it definitely had a kick, the way Tony and Sid's mom made it. "But we're used to cross-country," Matt said. "You know, flat ground?"

"Yeah. Iowa," Sid said.

"Iowa," Tony replied. "We've never skied in the mountains."

"It's better," Sid explained. "And easier. If you can handle that crap Midwest snow and ice, you can ski anywhere."

"Yeah," Tony said, shoving a gob of lamb in his mouth, bolting it down like a dog. "But these are the mountains, right? We should probably warm up on some bunny hills or something." Another giant scoop of basmati rice followed; it was almost transfixing to watch how fast Tony could eat. "Well, at least you should, Matt."

"I've skied more than you," Matt said.

"Yes, but who's the natural athlete here?"

Matt tore a piece away from the round pancake of garlic naan. "Sinking three-pointers blindfolded doesn't make you a better athlete. It just makes you a freak."

"Says you." Tony grinned and went back to inhaling his lunch.

"Yeah, says me." Matt shook his head, knowing that Tony did have some weird athletic prowess, at least when it came to anything with hand-eye coordination. He almost never missed a shot in basketball, destroyed Matt in ping-pong, beat him in golf, tennis, and racquetball.

But if they played long enough and hard enough, Matt would win. Matt knew deep down what he lacked in skill he made up for in stamina. Surely that had more to do with being athletic. He was persistent. *Tenacious.* That was the word his teachers used to describe him, and for many years he considered it a compliment. *Matt is very tenacious.* At the same time, he wondered why he couldn't have been graced with just a little natural talent—to even the playing field. Literally.

"We'll see," Tony said, shrugging.

"So," Matt turned to Sid. "What's this alpine touring, then?"

"It's like a combo of downhill and cross-country."

Tony frowned. "How?"

"You hike in," Sid explained. "You can snowshoe, or use these special skins to put on the skis." He held up a finger to catch the waitress's attention, which wasn't hard for Sid, because all the girls (and at least one waiter) had been glancing at him since they sat down in the booth. "Sid got his mother's looks," Mr. Jain liked to joke, "and Tony got my bunions."

"Skins?" Matt pictured snake hides wrapped around skis. "Hiking I understand, but I've never snowshoed." Out the window, a few blocks off Pearl Street, the Flatirons were visible, rising up from the green field like the back of some gigantic half-buried dragon.

"The skins go over the skis, so you can go forward but you won't slip back," Sid said. "Works great."

"And you've done this before?" Tony opened his wallet, pulled out a ten, hesitated, and then pulled out another.

"Yeah, a few times. There's nothing quite like skiing down pristine virgin powder." Sid conveniently emphasizing the word *virgin* just as the waitress arrived with water. She looked at each of them in turn, but kept her smile for Sid.

"Anything else?" She fluttered her eyes rapidly, ignoring Tony and Matt. The way she said *anything* started a heated tingle in Matt's lower intestines. Or maybe it was the chicken korma.

"No thanks." Sid flashed his movie star smile. "Just the check, please."

The waitress bit her lip with a nod, slid the bill to the middle of the table, and retreated to the bar.

"Kee-riiist!" Tony exhaled thickly when she was out of range. "I think she wanted to give you a lot more than the check." He peeked his head over the booth, checking the way her black T-shirt rose up from her jeans as she pulled down a glass from a shelf on the bar, revealing a small tattoo on her lower back, something with wings, or was it vines? "Oh man," he whispered. "Is that a tramp stamp?"

"Calm down, boner." Sid pulled out his own wallet to add money to the pile. "There's gonna be a party later. Plenty of ladies coming."

"A party?"

"My friend Dylan's having a party at his house."

"College girls?" Tony's face puckered, both in excitement and fear.

"They prefer to be called *women*," Sid said. "You know, because they are."

Matt threw a twenty on the table, knowing there wouldn't be a girl or woman who'd glance in their direction as long as Sid was around—which Matt found bewildering, since Sid sure didn't have any girlfriends in high school. At least, none he knew about.

Tony said as much. "Since when did you become such a stud?"

Sid shrugged into his jacket. "Since I stopped trying so hard."

"You weren't trying at all," Matt told him, wondering what combination of confidence and indifference would work on getting (and keeping) a girl's attention. So far, he hadn't found it. The indifference he was good at, or at least the impression of indifference. The confidence was another story. He didn't even know where to begin trying to fake that.

"That's the trick, grasshopper," Sid replied. "That *is* the trick."

MATT

Location: Boulder, Colorado
Elevation: 5,430 feet

"Nice place, Sid."

"Thanks."

"I was kidding," said Tony, peering at the ceiling and its collection of mysterious stains. "This place is a dump."

Sid tossed his keys on the coffee table, unoffended. "Boulder's expensive."

"It smells like old people."

Matt didn't think it looked all that bad, but he agreed there was an odor hanging in the air that reminded him of the nursing home his grandmother lived in—Cedar Winds Assisted Living, although there was nothing about the place that smelled like cedar, unless you counted pine-scented disinfectant. "So where are we sleeping, Sid?"

"In my room, I guess."

Tony wrinkled his nose. "I'm not sharing a bed."

Sid ignored him. "And someone can sleep on the couch."

"Ugh," said Tony, as if that was a worse option, and threw his duffel bag on said couch, narrowly missing a dark gray tabby cat that at first glance was so round and motionless it resembled a fuzzy throw pillow. The cat didn't move, except to open one jewel-green eye. A low growl rippled out.

"You can stay in a hotel if you don't like it, cheap ass."

"No way," said Tony. "I spent enough money on the plane ticket out here."

Sid laughed, went into the kitchen, and opened the refrigerator. "You sound just like Dad, you know," he called back. "He's a cheapskate too." He returned holding three cans of beer.

Tony took one. "I prefer the word *frugal*."

"So how long have you lived here?" Matt asked as he offered his hand to the cat, which sniffed it disinterestedly, and, finding nothing offensive, went back to its nap.

Sid tossed another beer to Matt. "Since last summer. Carter, my roommate, and his sister, Leah, needed another tenant after the last one moved out."

"Sister, huh?" Tony stared up at the ceiling, trying to find her room using X-ray vision. "Hot sister?"

Sid cracked open his beer. "Too hot for you, punk."

"What, she your girlfriend or something?"

"No," he said solemnly, sounding disappointed. "She's not my girlfriend."

"Ah, so fair game, then?"

"Of course." Sid smiled at his beer, foreseeing the

outcome. Matt foresaw it too—if this Leah chick wasn't interested in Sid, she certainly wouldn't be interested in his spazzy little brother.

"Are they here?" Matt asked, feeling as though he should ask permission before making himself comfortable.

"Nah," Sid said. "They're probably already at Dylan's. He's the one who'll hook us up with all the ski equipment tomorrow." He gave Tony a look, a once-over that seemed to leave him unsatisfied, searching for the right thing to say. "So don't be a dick, okay. He's saving us a ton of money by not having to rent all the stuff."

"Dylan?" Tony snorted. "With a name like that I bet he's a total stoner."

"You got it." Sid laughed. "Skis aren't the only things he can hook us up with. He's a total TFB with an endless supply."

"TFB?"

"Trust fund baby," Sid said. "I guess he's from a wealthy family out in Connecticut. Some richy-rich place in Hartford. Parents bought him a house in Boulder. Never seen the kid work, except he worked for a bit at the same sporting goods store with Carter. But he has an endless supply of money."

"Sounds like a douche."

"No. Not at all." Sid shook his head. "He's a great guy. And he's smart, too, but he just doesn't live in our orbit. It honestly never occurs to him *not* to have enough money."

"Wow," Tony said.

"The upside is he throws great parties."

The clock on the wall read ten to five. "Well, what are we waiting for?"

"Don't you want to shower and change?" Matt asked, mainly because he himself wanted to shower and change. He smelled of plane and unwashed masses. Or maybe it was just him.

"Why?"

"Girls, remember?" Sid reminded him.

"Oh yeah. Girls." Tony snatched his duffel bag, ruffled the cat's head, and then feigned surprise when it hissed and tried to bite his hand. "Nice cat you got there."

"It's a cat, Tony," Matt said. "Not a dog."

"Shower's upstairs," Sid said. "First door on the right."

Tony gave them a blank yet defiant stare before heading upstairs. Each wooden step creaked in protest.

Sid pushed off from the wall to seat himself in a threadbare recliner the color of rust. The cat watched him through slitted eyes and yawned. "Nuance escapes my brother."

"Yep, I've noticed." Matt took a swig of beer. It wasn't particularly cold, but tasted much better than the Old Milwaukee he and Tony stole from the fridge in Tony's dad's garage. He sat down next to the cat. "What's your name, baby?"

"His name is Marner," Sid informed him. "It's Leah's cat. And from what I've seen so far, an excellent judge of character."

"Marner," Matt said, immediately liking the name. He scratched the cat under the chin, and it pressed its head into his hand, purring loudly. "Like Silas Marner."

"Who?"

"It's a character from a book."

Sid blinked, confused. He was not a big reader of the classics, not into English literature, Matt realized. Since he was studying aerospace engineering, that made sense.

"So Tony tells me you were supposed to be going to spring training," Sid said, getting right to the point.

"Florida. Yeah."

Sid shook his head. "That sucks."

"Something came up," Matt said, wondering why he felt the need to explain. Why on Earth would he defend his dad? *Maybe because it was Sid.* He felt a quick stab of anger, and took a deep drink, trying to physically force it down his throat. Sid had the kind of dad you could depend on, the kind a kid was supposed to have, and he suddenly hated the fact that Sid and Tony, through no fault of their own, constantly reminded him of it.

"So," Matt continued, desperate to change the subject, "only a few more weeks and we'll graduate." Saying it out loud shocked him a little. In two months high school would be over. "Maybe things will get better in college."

Sid smiled, misinterpreting his meaning. "Of course. In college you'll be beating off girls with a stick." He glanced up at the ceiling, hearing a loud thump coming from the upstairs bathroom. "Or, like Tony, just beating off."

Matt laughed, but a large part of him refused to believe things were going to change that dramatically. "Some people say the high school years are the best ones of your life." Matt didn't know who said that, or why they would say that (especially if they actually had been through high school), but he'd heard it before. It wouldn't have surprised him if his father thought it; maybe that was the reason for his supreme dissatisfaction with his life. Satisfied people don't leave their families in search of a better one.

"Those people are certified morons." Sid drained the rest of the beer and crumpled his can. "It gets a lot better. Believe me. I know."

"One man's great thinker is another person's moron."

Sid laughed. "Oh man, that's a great one! Who said that?"

"Umberto Eco."

"Never heard of him. Some sort of genius, I bet."

"Philosopher," Matt replied. "Another writer." He wondered what college would really be like, which immediately reminded him of his college applications and the final decision he needed to make in the next few weeks. Where to spend the next four (to six) years. He hadn't applied to many schools, certainly not UC Boulder like Tony, who also applied to University of Iowa, Northwestern, and Drake. Matt's grades were good but not outstanding, and he took the ACT three times to get a high score of twenty-seven, only to have his dad remind him that a thirty was the type of score that college recruiters were looking for. Matt knew he wasn't the type of person who got recruited for anything, except maybe into the armed forces, but when he reminded his dad of that, his dad made a disgusted sound in his throat and said, "Well, that's up to you, isn't it?"

So far Matt didn't believe there was much in life that was up to him, but he didn't say that to his dad. There weren't going to be any awards or scholarships (sports or academic), seeing as he ranked 127 out of 651 students, and couldn't off the top of his head compute what percentage that was—another reason he didn't apply to a school like Northwestern. He did apply to the University of Iowa (not yet replied), the University of Minnesota (accepted), the University of Wisconsin (rejected), and Iowa State (wait-list). None of the schools were out of the Midwest, and he wondered if that was another mistake.

Tony bounded down the stairs, hair dripping wet and reeking with body spray that smelled like a sinus-clearing combination of cinnamon, clove, and pine sap. "I think I may have used up all the hot water," he told Sid, and grimaced at Matt. "I mean, it lasted all of three minutes and the water pressure totally sucks."

Matt knew this was his friend's version of an apology. "No problem." Matt headed upstairs, realizing that after all the heated conversations in the past week, a cold shower might be a welcome change.

By the time everyone had showered and changed, a sliver of moon hung over them in the clear violet sky. As they made their way to Dylan's, which turned out to be a mile-long hike up a steep drive, Matt wondered what the view would be like from the top of an actual mountain, someplace so high the curvature of the Earth was visible.

Around the next bend a modern, square box house with steel panels and a lot of mirrored glass appeared above a tall, muted green hedge of spruce. Matt followed Tony and Sid through the side gate, past the manicured boxwoods to the oversize front door.

"Rich boy lives here?" Tony whispered while Sid rapped his knuckles twice. From the outside everything was quiet, but a steady thump of music drifted through the door. Sid tried the handle and opened it.

"Ding dong, where's the bong?" Tony grinned.

"Okay"—Sid shut the door behind them—"please do me a favor and don't embarrass me."

"How could I do that, big bro? I'm just being myself."

"I know," Sid told him. "That's what I mean. Don't be yourself. Be someone else for a change."

"What? You want me to be like Matt? Stand in the corner all night, hanging out with the potted plants?"

Before Matt could think of a comeback, a petite, elfin-looking girl with short black hair appeared. She held a wine glass filled to the top with bloodred liquid. Wine, Matt guessed. Her lips were the same color. "Hey!" she waved, nearly sloshing the wine over the rim. "Sid! You're here!" She marched forward, barefoot, grinning like a maniac. Her skin-tight black jeans were ripped at the knee, and a low-cut Rockies T-shirt was covered by a cobalt-blue flannel shirt tied snugly around her hips.

Sid waggled his fingers, cheeks darkening into something Matt could have sworn was a blush. "Hey Julie."

She took a sip and swirled her glass thoughtfully, examining them from behind a thick layer of black eyeliner, eyes so dark blue they looked purple. "So who's your entourage this evening, Sid?"

"My brother, Tony, and his friend Matt."

"That's m-me," Tony stammered. "I mean, I'm Tony." He looked like he was in shock.

"Matt and Tony." Julie smiled benevolently. "How about a drink?"

She didn't wait for an answer, but turned back to the kitchen. "Beer's in the fridge. Everyone's outside at the pit."

They each grabbed one and made their way out back, through the sliding glass door and onto the deck. Immediately, the scent of marijuana greeted them.

"Hey Sid!" A tall, muscular guy, wearing a black UC baseball hat waved them over. "You made it."

"Hey Dylan."

So that's Dylan, thought Matt. Of course. He had a very Dylanesque look. When he removed his hat, he ran his hand through a thick curtain of wavy caramel-brown hair, the color and luster reminding Matt of a cocker spaniel. When Dylan smiled a set of dimples revealed themselves. His teeth looked like Chiclets, and even though it was only April, he was already tan. Dylan was the golden boy. "These your brothers?"

"Matt and Tony," Sid replied, not correcting him. "Visiting from Iowa."

"No kidding?" Dylan smoothed his hair once more and readjusted his hat. "Awesome. You guys play baseball?"

"No," Tony and Matt replied in unison, sounding like twins.

"Huh, I thought everyone in Iowa played baseball," Dylan said. "You know that line? Is this place heaven?"

"No, it's Iowa," Matt heard himself say. "*Field of Dreams.* Good movie."

Someone in the group—a girl—let out a giggle, a pixie laugh, but in the growing dark Matt couldn't see who it was.

"But they do ski," Sid added.

"We were just talking about that!" Dylan grinned. "Carter and I have been coming up with some sweet plans for this weekend. Berthoud Pass, man."

"Just dumped another two feet of fresh powder up there." A very skinny, very tall, freckled, redheaded guy informed them, and Matt assumed this was Carter, Sid's roommate. He looked around the group for his sister. *What was her name again?* he thought. *Leah? Or Mia?*

"Hey Sid, remember that day trip we took two weeks ago up there?" Dylan asked.

"Of course. I almost got stuck in a tree on that one run. Scared the crap out of me."

"Well, word on the street is there's an old cabin a few miles from that spot. Totally abandoned."

"Really? Where'd you hear that?"

"One of those old forest service guys told me about it," Dylan confided. "That old stoner Gary, the one who works at the ski shop. Said they used to have great parties out there back in the day. We should ski in, stay in the cabin overnight, and then do the loop back the next day."

"But how will you find it, if it's so secret?"

"He gave me coordinates." Dylan chugged back the rest of his beer.

"Coordinates?" Sid asked. "You mean like forty degrees north and thirty degrees west? Like spy stuff?"

"Exactly. He wrote it down, but I had to Google it to figure out how to do it," Dylan admitted. "I guess I can just put the numbers in my GPS, so it shouldn't be too hard."

"Wouldn't it be illegal, though?" Julie asked, coming up behind Dylan to ruffle his hair. *Of course,* Matt thought. *That makes sense. Julie is Dylan's girlfriend.* It was obvious as they stood next to each other. "Isn't that like breaking and entering?"

Everyone shifted slightly as Julie slid her way into the circle. Wedged between Dylan's broad shoulders and Carter's height, she looked even smaller.

"Well, I guess it's not locked up," Dylan said. "And it's not in RMNP either."

"RMNP?" Tony was confused.

"Rocky Mountain National Park," Dylan explained. "No, it's in the Arapaho National Forest."

"So how is that different?" Matt asked.

"Well, I guess the forest service land isn't maintained to the same level. According to this guy, there's a bunch of old abandoned lookout towers and stuff."

"Well," Julie said, "can I come?"

"Sure," Carter said quickly. "Of course." He took a swig from his bottle.

"Totally." Dylan nodded. "The more the merrier." He put his arm around her and squeezed. Carter glanced at them and took another long drink.

"Wait," Julie sighed, as if reminded of something unfortunate. "I don't know if I want to bunk with a bunch of guys in some rat-infested cabin."

"Hey Leah." Sid nodded at a girl opposite him. "Why don't you come with? You're one of the best skiers."

"Hey," Carter protested, "I'm the one who taught her everything she knows."

"And I thank you," Leah replied, "for being such a good teacher." She nodded at Sid. "Sure, it sounds like fun. I don't have anything going on this weekend."

"Awesome!" Dylan said. "Sounds like we have a plan."

Leah, Matt saw, was in many ways the physical opposite of Julie. Where Julie was petite and dark, Leah was pale and tall. Not as tall as her brother, but sturdier looking. Her bright red hair (more auburn than carrot) was wild with curls, leaping from her scalp as if in full retreat from her head. Milk-white skin, and freckles dusting the bridge of a nose that could only be described as *buttonish*. Only her eyes were dark—deep brown but lit from within. A glinting keenness that suggested intelligence. The type of eyes that didn't miss a thing. A small diamond stud earring in her left nostril flashed when it caught the firelight.

"Definitely. And besides"—Leah nodded to Julie—"we need to show these Iowans a good time, don't we?" She blinked at Matt (or was it a wink?), while a sly grin widened her mouth. After a few seconds Matt had to look away. College girls—at least these college girls—didn't play coy, and Matt couldn't decide if that was better or worse than what he was used to. Not that he was used to much. He'd only ever kissed one girl before, last year at a party, and that had been a dare. He never even knew her name. Was it Mandy? Molly? Something like that.

He drank down the rest of his beer, hoping for the combination of alcohol and elevation to smooth down the edges in his brain, quieting the incessant trivial chatter and loosening his muscles. Just make him relax. That was it; he just wanted to feel like a better version of himself. He examined the empty bottle, realized he was going to need more than one beer to achieve that goal, then excused himself and headed back to the house.

Leah followed him through the sliding door. "So what's your story, farm boy?"

"Huh?" Matt replied, grabbing a bottle from the fridge. "Uh, I live in the suburbs." He offered her another beer.

She shook her head with a grin, curls bouncing over her shoulders like springs. "You mean you don't have to get up and milk the cows every morning before school?"

"That's Wisconsin, not Iowa," he said, realizing she was joking. At least, he thought she was. "In Iowa we have to get up early to shuck corn and feed the pigs."

Leah giggled, and then Matt knew she was the one with the high, twinkly fairy laugh. It seemed strange; she didn't look like a giggler. "So are you the strong, silent type?" she wanted to know.

"Mostly silent." The temperature seemed to have dropped thirty degrees, and Matt didn't feel like making his way back out to the fire to get warm when he could just stay in the house. He retreated to the leather couch in the living room. "And cold." Everyone else was still at the fire, but the smell of all that pot was giving him a headache, which he thought was ironic, considering it was supposed to have the opposite effect.

"You like to ski?" Leah plopped down next to him on the couch, tucking her stockinged feet underneath her legs like a cat.

"Sure," he said. "Of course. Doesn't everyone?"

"Of course." She grinned back like she had just told him a dirty joke. "What else do you like to do?"

Despite his nice buzz, Matt blushed. "What do you mean?" He knew what she meant, but didn't wait for a reply. "By the way, thanks for letting us crash at your place."

"No problem. I figure any friend of Sid's . . ." She didn't finish, but Matt could feel her sizing him up. He wondered if she liked what she saw. His cheeks heated into a burn.

"I like your cat," he blurted, hoping she couldn't read his mind at that exact moment. He shifted awkwardly on the couch, unsure of how to arrange his arms and legs. He suddenly felt huge and bulky and aware of how much space he was occupying. Too much, it seemed.

"Really?" She was surprised. "No one likes that cat. He's such a turd, but I found him living in the restaurant Dumpster so I brought him home."

"Oh. I mean, I like his name. Marner. Silas Marner. From the book, right?"

"Yeah. Most people don't get that reference." She cocked her head sideways. "Well, at least most high school guys wouldn't."

"Oh." He wondered if that was a compliment. He hoped so. "Well, I like George Eliot. And I really like that story."

"My favorite author," Leah said quietly, looking somewhere over his shoulder, and when Matt turned and looked out the picture window he saw Tony stagger up the steps to the deck, laughing like a donkey. He was definitely past drunk.

"It looks like your friend's enjoying himself," Leah said.

"Yeah, he's an expert in that area."

They watched Tony take two steps, lean over, and nonchalantly spray a fountain of vomit into the junipers.

"Nice," Matt sighed. "Second time today."

"Maybe he'll go for a hat trick. The night is still young."

"I thought pot wasn't supposed to have that effect."

"It doesn't," Leah said. "But whiskey definitely does."

"I'd rather have a bottle in front of me than a frontal lobotomy," Matt replied.

"Oh yeah?" Leah arched an eyebrow. "Aren't you the clever one."

"No, not me." Matt pressed his bottle next to his cheek, if only to check the temperature coming off it. He wondered if he should switch to water; he sure didn't want to pull a Tony. Not in front of a girl like Leah. This was no time to get stupid. "That's Dorothy Parker."

"A guy who quotes women." Leah laughed and leaned forward, putting her hand on his knee. With a suggestive squeeze she smiled, her eyes sparkling as brightly as her diamond nose ring. "I *knew* there was a reason I liked you."

DAY 2

MATT
Location: Berthoud Pass
Elevation: 11,307 feet

Matt awoke that morning to the low hum of a ceiling fan slowly circling above him, and he discovered he was in the same place on the couch, except reclining and covered by a fuzzy blanket. He flexed his toes—his shoes were missing.

It was still dark. He fumbled around his pocket for his phone. 5:13 a.m. He was thirsty—the kind of thirsty that comes from too much smoke and too much booze. Tony was lying on the opposite couch, swaddled in his blanket like a giant newborn, while someone Matt didn't know—*Dave? Joe?*—snored lightly from the recliner. It appeared to be a slumber party, though he couldn't remember falling asleep.

He rubbed at the crick in his neck, trying to recall what happened after Tony barfed in the bushes.

A few things sprang to mind:

Taking a few drags off Dylan's bong.

Standing in the kitchen laughing, making peanut-butter-and-potato-chip sandwiches and drinking Dr Pepper.

Matt remembered eating three sandwiches and say-ing, "This is the best sandwich I've ever eaten in my life."

Tony replying, "I love the way food feels in my mouth."

Then Matt laughing like a hyena and shooting Dr Pepper out his nose.

And that was it. Although there was something about seeing Carter and Julie together in the hallway, something about the way they stood together, that Matt was sure he hadn't imagined. Carter's hand gripped Julie's elbow, their faces inches apart from each other—like they were retreat-ing from a kiss. Matt was looking for the bathroom, and as he stumbled down the hallway he heard Julie say, "We can't do this." Or was it "We can't do this again"? Matt weaved around the corner, causing Carter to shoot him a perturbed look and immediately drop Julie's arm. Matt thought about apologizing, first for being drunk and sec-ond for looking for the bathroom. Carter, by comparison, didn't look drunk at all, walking away with such a smooth quickness that Matt blinked and wondered if he'd only hallucinated the scene.

Apparently nothing else happened after that; at least nothing else embarrassing. Matt was certain he would remember anything humiliating—that was what his brain always recalled best. After a few minutes watching the sky lighten, his eyes didn't feel quite so dry and raw. He heard a dull thump upstairs, then a faint sound of water running. Part of him wanted to slip out the door, but he wasn't sure how to find his way back. He didn't even know the address.

"Wakey, wakey. Eggs and bakey." Dylan came in the living room carrying a grease-spotted bag.

"No wakey," Tony whispered from his swaddle.

Dave or Joe moaned from the chair.

"Let's get going, honey bunnies. The caravan's leaving in twenty."

"Why so early?" It wasn't even five thirty; Matt was never awake at this hour.

"We need to stock up supplies and get out there this morning," Dylan said. "We got bluebird sky today. No afternoon storms."

"So don't we have time?"

"It's a long hike," he added.

"Are you always like this?" Tony mumbled, eyes still closed.

Dylan grinned. "Work hard. Party hard. Play hard. That's the motto." He threw an egg-and-bacon sandwich at Tony's head like a grenade. "We already partied hard. Now it's time to play."

But it seemed to Matt that they were about to "play" harder than they partied. Berthoud Pass turned out to be an actual pass through the mountains, a twisting, snaking two-lane highway that crossed the Continental Divide. Matt watched the signs on Highway 40 and felt his ears pop as they ascended.

"What's the Continental Divide again?" Tony asked

from the backseat of Carter's van. Matt rode shotgun. Sid drove with Dylan, Julie, and Leah, so they ended up with Carter and the mystery machine.

"So on the east side of the mountains the rivers flow to the Gulf of Mexico and the Atlantic." Carter scratched the hairy stubble on his face. With the morning sunlight streaming through the windshield, it made a strange orange halo around his chin. "But on the west side, the water flows to the Pacific."

"Weirdness." Tony sipped his Gatorade, contemplating the mysteries of geology.

"So you've been up here before?" Matt asked Carter, who drove as though he was eighty years old and legally blind. Slow, yet disturbingly aggressive. But it was a narrow highway with U-turn switchbacks, so Matt decided speed was not a plus in this situation.

"Oh yeah," Carter said. "Just last weekend with Sid and my sister, but we hung out on the bunny hills. Not like what Dylan's got planned."

"Bunny hills? Really?"

"Yeah, at Old Terrain Park. The place used to be an actual ski resort."

"But it's not anymore?"

"They closed it down about ten years ago," Carter said. "Took all the lifts and signs and stuff down, so now it's totally wild again."

"Wild?" Matt tried not to sound nervous, but Carter's driving made him want to shut his eyes and hum. Instead, he grabbed the dashboard when Carter slammed his brakes as a herd of deer galloped across the highway, flew over a ditch, and disappeared into the pines.

"Whoa," Tony said. "That *is* wild."

"Saw a bear out here once," Carter told them. "But that was last summer when I was hiking up in Estes. She had two cubs with her, and I thought I was going to bite it that time."

"What happened?"

"I backed up real slow, sat down, and pulled my jacket over my head," Carter said grimly. "Thankfully she ran off with her cubs."

"That's amazing." Tony laughed.

"Didn't feel amazing when it happened. Just felt terrifying."

They drove on, the van groaning up the road, until after a few more miles the ground leveled out. Ahead, a large brown building came into view, an oval parking lot on one side of the highway.

"There's the base lodge." Carter turned into the lot, and Matt counted ten cars, mostly SUVs and the all-popular Subarus. The air was cold and clear, but the sun, now fully up, was promising warmth. The sky was the dictionary definition of the word *blue*—perfect skiing weather. For the first time in a week Matt felt something that reminded him of happiness.

"Tony! Matt!" Sid waved. "C'mon and get your stuff!"

Twenty minutes later, outfitted with poles, boots, and

bindings, they stared up at a hill of snow. Not a mountain, Matt realized, but a hill. A very steep one. Technically they were already in the mountains; they were surrounded by them, the peaks rising and falling away into the horizon like giant mounds of whipped cream. The hill ahead was clear of trees, but thick green swaths of pine fanned down on either side, defining a wide alley of snow in the middle. That was what Matt could not get over: the sheer amount and depth of the snow, the brightness of it, so white and dazzling he had to pull down his goggles to prevent blindness. He took great gulps of the thin air, trying to get the oxygen to his muscles as fast as possible. He was going to need all the help he could get.

"Okay," Sid said, "let's take a practice hike up. Get used to the skins."

"Got it." Dylan, Leah, Carter, and Julie had already started up, and Sid followed in the track they'd made. Matt thought it felt similar to all the other times he skied cross-country, and in a few steps the glide came back. Sid was right about the snow—the skis floated, not scraping on slushy ice. It was as smooth as talcum powder. The green nylon skins hooked onto the tip and tail of his skis, covering the bottoms, reminding Matt of thin pieces of nubby carpet. And to his surprise, they did work, preventing him from backsliding as he climbed. But it was still exhausting. Within a minute he was sweating. After five minutes he realized the hill was much longer than it looked. His thighs burned; so did his calves. *Forget it,* Matt thought. This was not at all like cross-country, and it certainly wasn't easier with the gear he carried on his back like a pack mule.

"Good God," Tony grunted behind him. "I thought this was supposed to be fun."

"We're out of shape," Matt wheezed the obvious, his head pounding with every pulse of blood. He leaned on his poles, and even though he inhaled as fast as he could, it felt useless. His lungs shuddered and burned as though he was drowning. Hot, sharp stabs radiated through his back—tiny knives of fire poking under his rib cage. He was in no way ready for this. "Now I know what it feels like to have asthma."

Tony struggled up next to him, panting like a dog. Sid glanced back, apologetic. "We're over eleven thousand feet right now." Sweat gleamed on his forehead. "I forget what it's like the first time up here."

"What it's like is that it totally sucks." Tony coughed.

"Just a bit more." Sid pointed his pole to the ridgeline where everyone was already camped out, waiting for them. "It will be worth it on the way down, I swear."

Matt nodded, too weak to argue. They were more than halfway up, so they might as well keep going. *Ba da dum strum strum.* A banjo tune vibrated against his leg. Cell phone. Text message from his dad. The first time in over a week he had heard anything from him. Considering the last conversation they'd had, Matt figured his dad wanted a cooling off period.

He felt his anger return as he climbed. Of course his father would text right at the moment when Matt had stopped thinking about him and what he had told him over the phone, the *real* reason he wasn't going to be in Florida, the reason his mother already knew about but Tony and Sid did not. Matt knew they would find out eventually. After all, his mom was still good friends with the Jains. But he didn't think he could tell Tony. For some reason, he was afraid if he did he would start crying. And now his father was texting him. Like he had some weird sixth sense. Somehow he knew Matt was having fun—if you can call climbing up a mountain of snow fun—and it was his mission to ruin it.

"Dammit," he exhaled, not wanting to check his phone. *Not yet.* He figured if he stopped now he'd fall over. The phone repeated its banjo strum once more, but Matt ignored it. Instead, he concentrated on moving forward, moving up, mimicking Sid's motions. Head down, knees bent, shoulders loose, right foot, left foot. Glide, glide, inhale, exhale.

When they arrived at the summit Matt felt like someone who'd just got punched in the kidneys. His legs were a quivering mess of exhausted muscle. If he fell down now he figured he'd never get back up.

"Ooof!" Tony did fall down, splaying out into a drift like he'd been shot in the back. "That was NOT a bunny hill."

"That's because you climbed it." Dylan laughed. "Don't

worry. You guys did good. Most newbies take a lot longer." He glanced back at Carter, Julie, Leah, and Sid. "Isn't that right, Carter?"

"You know it." Carter smiled, appearing less like he'd just hiked the same route and more like he'd ridden a gondola to the top. "It took months before I got used to it."

"That doesn't make me feel much better," Matt said. His eyes were pounding so hard he was afraid they might pop. He pulled out his bottle of water and drank half, hoping that would ease the hammering in his head.

"Maybe that will." Carter gestured to the view in front of them. "Not bad!"

When Matt's heart rate dropped to somewhere near normal, his vision cleared and he raised his head. It was endless—a sea of blue and white before him. An ocean in the sky. The immensity of it gripped him with the dizzying effect of being unable to sense where the Earth ended and the sky began. It was beautiful.

But terrifying. A pressing white noise filled the space around him now that everyone had gone silent, a roar the mountains made. Matt felt like he was ten years old again, seeing the ocean for the first time, watching the relentless waves pound the rocks. Only one thought surfaced:

I am a little speck of nothing.

"Take it in!" Dylan's laugh was a boom, echoing across the ridge. "The mountains are calling and I must go!"

"John Muir," Matt said, trying not to gasp.

"Awesome." Dylan smiled, seeming like the type who

used the word *awesome* a lot. And meant it. "You even know John Muir."

"This kid's one of those quotable weirdoes," Tony explained. "Has a giant quote book with everything in it. Nerd memorized them all."

"Oh yeah?" Leah asked him, curious. She pushed her goggles up her forehead; her cheeks wore matching pink splotches and her mouth was a deeper slash of crimson, shining with cherry ChapStick. Like her brother, she appeared unfazed by the climb, and she watched Matt curiously, seemingly unmoved by the view. Matt guessed she'd seen it many times. "How about this: I am so clever that sometimes I don't understand a single word of what I am saying."

"That one's easy," Matt said, knowing the answer immediately. "Oscar Wilde." Oscar Wilde had several pages of quotes in his giant quote book, and every one of them had been a winner.

Leah laughed. "Well, color me impressed."

"Which way do we go now?" Tony asked, stripping off the nylon skins and rolling them up. Matt sat down next to him and did the same, popping them off in quick succession.

"We go down the other side." Carter adjusted his goggles and pulled his hat down over his ears, which looked as red as his hair. "End up at the little bowl off to the right." He glanced at Dylan, who agreed. "We'll take that first marked trail east to the second ridge." Then

Carter dug in his poles, shoved off, and vanished into the white. Dylan, Julie, and Sid followed, cutting wide, swooping arcs into the snow.

"Well, okay then." Tony needed no more hints. "See you at the bottom, dude."

Matt balanced his ski tips over the edge and watched the rest of them fly down the hill. It was disconcerting, he finally realized, because he was looking for flags, for signs, for some sort of marker to tell him where to go. But there were none.

"Are you ready, Matt?" Leah stood next to him, tucking her red curls down the back of her parka.

"I think so." He gripped his poles and pushed down, lifting the skis up with a step forward. He hesitated slightly as he followed Tony's trail, wondering how to avoid rocks and trees and God knows what else that could be hiding below the surface. All the white was a glare, messing with his depth perception, starting a trickle of panic in his limbs. He turned sharply, making a thick gust of powder, which only blew back in his face. He knew he was going slow, but he was intimidated about which track to follow. Still, it was fun, and a million times better than the climb up.

"You're doing it wrong!" Leah shouted, swooping past him. She waved her pole to stop.

"What?" Matt slid to a halt. He thought he was skiing down a mountain—how was he doing it wrong?

"You're following Tony's line."

"I'm not supposed to? I don't want to hit anything."

"You won't," Leah explained, shaking her head. "The snow is deep. Really deep."

"I don't know. . . ." Matt looked at the trees off to the side. *How deep could it be?*

"The whole point of this is to go where no one's gone before."

"That's a *Star Trek* quote," Matt informed her.

"Exactly." Leah grinned, and with that grin Matt felt his heart squeeze a little harder. She smiled at him the way he'd always hoped a pretty girl would. Like he was the only person in the universe. "So let's boldly go where no one has. It'll be great, I promise."

He watched the track she left as she continued down, the movement downright hypnotic, and after a few seconds he followed, skiing next to the trail she made but not in it.

She was right. He seemed to float above the snow, almost hovering, and for the next twenty seconds he flew, hearing nothing but the *schuss* of drifts around him, even forgetting that every single muscle in his legs had been worked to the point of combustion.

And then he was down, carving sharply right, digging in the edges to a tight hockey stop. Twenty minutes up and two minutes to the bottom.

"Now that's what I'm talking about!" Dylan hooted with glee, slapping his gloves together in a proud smack.

"What?"

"Your face, man!"

"My face?" Matt's face hurt, and he touched his glove to his cheek, wondering if he got smacked by something and didn't notice. "What's wrong with it?"

"Absolutely nothing," Carter said. "But you're grinning like an idiot."

"Oh." That's why his cheeks hurt. From smiling. He hadn't done that in a while.

"Dude! That was the sweetest ride," Tony exclaimed. "Better than sex."

"Not if you're doing it right," Sid deadpanned, and Julie laughed knowingly. Everyone did, even Tony, who as far as Matt knew was still a complete virgin. Just like he was. He finally pulled out his phone. Two texts from his dad. Great.

Call me back!

Need to talk to u!

Of course, thought Matt, *now he wants to talk.* He held the phone up, but there wasn't a strong signal, and the last text he'd sent was yesterday afternoon to let his mother know he arrived. He typed another one to both of them.

Ski today. Berthoud Pass. Fun!

That should be enough information. He typed a separate text to his dad.

Ok. Will call L8R.

There, he thought, turning off his phone to save the battery. *Let him sit around and wait for a change.*

"Think the newbies can handle Current Creek?" Carter asked.

"Think so." Dylan nodded.

"Where's that?" Tony asked. The downhill run seemed to have recharged him. He no longer looked exhausted and hungover.

"There." Sid pointed over Tony's head at the line of mountains a few miles in the distance.

"North and west, my newbies." Dylan held up his GPS. "The magic numbers to the cabin are thirty-nine degrees, fifty-one minutes, forty-four seconds north; one hundred and five degrees, fifty-three minutes, and twenty-nine seconds west."

"What does that even mean?" Julie leaned back on her poles, scanning the horizon. "Sounds like we're searching for buried treasure."

"Don't really know," Dylan said. "But I'm ready to find out."

THE HUNTER
Location: Seven miles northeast of the ski group

The cat, like the old saying, was curious. It was early and the morning air was heavy with scent. Bark and leaf and stone. Ice and snow. Fur and feather. One scent in particular turned its head, an aroma the animal had never smelled before. Wet wool, something chemical and foreign, but also the pungent whiff of sweat and body heat. Another animal.

The lion was young, rangy and lean, only its third spring in the mountains. It was also hungry. One small rabbit the day before had not offered much of a meal, and the cat huffed the breeze deeply, mouth open, tasting the air. There was something out there, and the cat switched directions, turning west against the morning light. It did not take long for it to find the tracks this strange new animal left, and it quickened its pace through the trees, finally on the hunt.

MATT

Location: Ridge west of Current Creek
Elevation: 11,500 feet

"How you doing, Matt?" Dylan unzipped his pack, digging around for his lunch.

"Better," he huffed, easing himself down onto a drift next to Tony, who was already devouring his sandwich. "Much better." The morning had passed quickly, and now the sun was so warm that if he closed his eyes and tilted his face up, he would swear he was on a beach somewhere, not surrounded by ice. He tried not to look at Tony's food; his stomach growled in protest.

"You guys are naturals," Dylan added. "Good form."

"This elevation is kicking my butt, though."

"Yeah. Drink more water." Dylan handed him a banana, two turkey-and-Swiss sub sandwiches, and a bag of chips. "We'll take it easy for the rest of the afternoon." He checked his GPS and squinted. "We're only about a mile or two from the cabin now."

"Good." Matt exhaled, trying not to rip into the bag of

chips like a wild dog. In the past year he had given up junk food, but reasoned it was okay if he was on vacation. Plus, he'd gone up and down mountains all morning. Surely one bag of chips wouldn't send him back into a downward spiral of hoarding food under his bed. He wasn't twelve anymore. He had some self-control. "Thanks," he said, forcing the thought away. "I'm starving."

"No kidding!" Tony added, licking the salt from the inside of his chip bag. "I don't know the last time I've ever been that hungry." He crumpled the bag, and along with his banana peel, shoved all the garbage into the empty sub wrapper and wadded it into a ball. "At least, not since this morning."

"All the fresh air, I bet." Dylan laughed and tromped away. Matt shook his head, undid his bindings, and wiggled his toes around in his boots. He ate the banana first, letting it melt on his tongue, then moved on to the chips. He ate each one slowly, thin wafers dissolving into salt in his mouth. Nothing had ever tasted this good before, and all too soon, the bag was empty.

The sun was hot at this elevation, bright and insistent. Rays of light glittered off the snow pack like a field of diamonds. They were perched on a ridgeline a few hundred yards above the trees, and from this vantage point Matt felt like he was on Mount Olympus, looking down on all the mortals below. The only mortal thing he saw was the dark outline of a bird coming down for a landing in the treetops. Even from this distance it looked large. *An eagle.*

Despite reminding himself to take his time, he demolished the first sandwich in five bites. Thirsty, he scooped a wad of snow into his mouth, which tasted like copper or some tarnished metal, sweet with minerals. To him it was delicious, and he guessed it was about as clean as water gets.

"Don't eat the yellow snow," Tony reminded him. "Or the brown."

"Thanks, Einstein."

"Did Einstein say that one?" Tony was serious.

"No, Tony."

"My head hurts," Tony continued. "My eyeballs hurt, my legs hurt, my lungs hurt, even my ass hurts. Pretty much everything hurts."

"Just wait till tomorrow." Matt chewed his snowball. "It'll be even worse."

"Ugh. Don't remind me. After this trip I'm going to really need a vacation."

Matt pulled out his phone, switched it on, and held it up—the signal was stronger up here. "My dad finally texted me." He turned it off, tucking it back into his chest pocket. He fought the urge to check it. He didn't care, he reminded himself, what his dad had written.

"Oh yeah? Nice," Tony said, somewhat sarcastically. "So what did he say this time?"

"Same old crap," Matt lied. "Work shit, I don't know. Trying to apologize and promising to make it up to me."

"Of course." Tony snorted. "He's just trying to jerk you around. As usual."

Matt didn't answer.

"You gonna call back?" Tony ate his own snowball, after carefully checking that it was completely pristine. "I wouldn't do it, dude."

"I don't know." The battery was already half out of juice. "I guess I will later."

"Let him stew a little longer. Or better yet, take a picture of the two smoking hot babes and send it to him. Let him know how much fun you're having." Tony's grin was evil. "Knowing him, he'll probably be jealous." Matt figured Tony had heard the stories before, mainly by eavesdropping on his parents, who found out from other neighbors, how Matt's dad had left his mom for a twenty-two-year-old college student. Matt's dad was a professor of psychology (of all things), yet somehow didn't get the memo that he was just another middle-aged guy with a paunch and the misbelief that having an affair with a young woman would somehow prevent him from getting old and dying. Classic textbook case, Matt thought.

Matt's dad left six years ago, moving first to an apartment in downtown Des Moines and then to a condo that he shared with the then–twenty-two-year-old Shannon, was now twenty-eight. No one thought that would last, and even though it had been six years, up until last week Matt had still held out hope his parents would reconcile. That his dad would move back in and things would go back to the way they were. He squeezed his second sandwich flat, fingers puncturing right through the bread, remembering his dad's news, and all that hope suddenly drained out, leaving an empty pit in his stomach no amount of food could fill.

"Look, Matt," Tony continued. "I know he's your dad and everything . . ." He sighed. "Just don't let him off so easy. Don't let him walk all over you."

"I know." Matt stared at his sandwich, wanting to eat it, but decided it would be smarter to wait. "And I don't let him walk all over me," he said quietly, not wanting to believe that's what Tony really thought—that like his name, he was something to wipe your feet on. But what his best friend said made sense, as if the lack of oxygen had increased Tony's brain cells. *He should hang out on mountaintops more often.*

Carter trudged over, all loaded up, carrying a long pole and a shovel. "We'll be heading out in about an hour."

"Where you going?"

"Gonna check the snowpack on this ridge." He waved the pole to the higher peak rising up on the left side. "We'll be heading down that way."

"What's that?" With Carter's coat unzipped, Matt saw what appeared to be a large stopwatch strapped to his chest.

"My AV beacon," Carter answered. "I always have a shovel, snow probe, and my beacon." He blinked at Tony and Matt as if they were idiots. "Didn't Dylan give you one?"

Tony pulled his out. "Sid gave me one."

"I don't have one," Matt said, a bit squeaky with the sudden fear that everyone else knew way more than he did.

Carter sighed, stabbing his pole down. "Dylan can be a bit of a stoner." He shook his head. "And not in a good way. Hang on, Matt." He stomped over to where Julie and Dylan were sunning themselves near a large granite rock, sunglasses on.

They watched Carter gesture accusingly to Dylan, and though they didn't hear everything being said, the words *dumbass, hell, snow, ice, transmitter, BC,* and *what the fuck?* were blatantly clear.

"Well, Carter sounds pissed," Tony whispered. "What's *BC* mean?"

"I don't know," Matt said, panic swelling in his chest. "Uh, *backcountry?*"

Carter came back with another transmitter. "Here." He tossed it to Matt—a small black plastic knob on a corded necklace. Matt turned it over in his hands, reading the word **TRACKER2** on the front.

"It's already set to transmit, so just wear it under your jacket," Carter explained.

"Thanks." Matt slipped it over his neck and nestled it against his thermal shirt. "Doesn't Dylan need one?"

"Yeah, but Dylan doesn't mind."

Matt nodded, seeing the nonchalant way Dylan tossed it over to Carter, smiling and laughing and waving him off.

Carter clipped into his skis and adjusted his goggles

and gloves. He leaned back and looked up, his eyes searching the empty sky as if the explanation to something would be found up there. "It's always amazing to me how smart people can be so stupid." He pushed off toward the ridge with a grunt.

Matt smiled. The more time he spent with Carter, the more he liked him.

"All right, my newbies!" Dylan jumped to his feet, waving his arms like a television preacher. "Time to cruise! We gotta get a few more runs in before we lose this day!"

When Matt stood up, something popped in his back. He groaned and cracked his neck.

"God, you're old," Tony said. "You sound like my dad does after shooting hoops."

The last thing Matt wanted was a reminder that Tony's dad played basketball with him in the driveway every weekend. He watched Leah bend over and clip into her skis, red curls shining like fire against her green parka. He had wanted to go over and talk to her during lunch, but she sat down next to Julie, heads tilted together in such a way that it seemed to be a private conversation.

"So what's the deal with Leah?"

"Huh? What deal?" Tony wrinkled his face, then squinted in their direction. "What do you mean?"

"Nothing." Matt remembered how Sid had said Leah wasn't his girlfriend, and also how disheartened Sid had seemed by that fact. But maybe he was still trying, Matt thought wryly, wondering if Sid was tenacious. He seriously doubted it. Things had always come easy for Sid. And the only problem with everything being so easy, Matt noted, was that you had no idea what to do when it got hard.

"She's hot," Tony admitted. "And I think she likes you."

"Really? You think?"

"Well, she doesn't seem repulsed."

"Thanks."

"No problemo." Tony eyed Matt's sandwich. "You gonna eat that?"

"Later." Matt folded the bag back around it. "Anyway, she probably has a boyfriend."

"Probably." Tony stared at his sub like a dog until Matt shoved it back in his pack. "But I don't see him anywhere."

"What does that mean?"

"Whatever you want it to, dude." Tony leaned back and closed his eyes against the sunlight. "Whatever you want it to."

The snow was golden, turning as orange and pink as sherbet in the setting sun.

"This run will take us down through the bowl," Dylan told Matt, the wide clearing spread out a mile down below them, encircled by thick forest. "The whole run is about three miles total, and then from the bottom we should be able to ski over to the cabin."

"Great." Matt was so tired his legs trembled. He

glanced back at Carter, who was perched on a large snow slab two hundred yards up. Carter pointed his pole at something, then back at Leah, Tony, and Julie, who were in line behind him.

"What's he waiting for?" Sid asked, leaning over his poles next to Matt.

Exhausted, Matt shrugged. "No clue." *We have to be close to the cabin*, he thought, feeling proud he'd handled the whole day without collapsing or completely embarrassing himself.

"C'mon dude!" Dylan hollered. "Go, already!"

Carter shouted something back, before sliding forward into a slow curve over the drift. He carved one complete *S* before a huge circle splintered around him, cracking open and dropping like a giant sinkhole—with Carter disappearing right into it.

"What the . . . ," Matt began.

"No!" Dylan spun around, grabbed Matt's shoulder, and shoved him forward. "Get out of here!"

"W-w-what?" He stared over Dylan's shoulder trying to figure out where Carter had gone.

"Snow slide!"

"A snow . . . ?"

"Avalanche!"

The word didn't register immediately. Like a foreign language with a certain translational lag time, it took Matt a second to process the meaning. Fifty yards above them an enormous white cloud billowed, as if something had just exploded. And the plume increased, growing larger and wider as it raced down the slope. It roared like a jumbo jet.

"Go!" Dylan screamed, startling him forward. "Head for those trees!"

Matt could see Sid, already a hundred yards away, going straight downhill. He followed, keeping his tips pointed and parallel, hoping gravity would work in his favor. *How fast am I going?* he wondered. *Thirty miles an hour? Forty?* The wind whipped tears from his eyes—he'd forgotten to put on his goggles.

The trees were approaching fast. He was coming at a dead run.

Dead run, thought Matt. *A dead run. This is a dead run.*

He was trying to outrun death. Literally.

His tip caught in a soft patch of slush and he careened wildly to the right, dangerously close to a lodgepole pine. A branch slapped him in the face, knocking his chin up. *Smack!* Hard as a two-by-four, and the force spun him around. Backward now, the ground rose underneath him, a wave of snow blowing up beneath his feet. Something snapped, plastic cracking—his skis broke free from the boots, his poles struck out blindly. There was no time to scream, only primal reflexes, and he flailed and bicycled his limbs like a swimmer trying to reach the surface. But this water was frozen, solid as cement. It surrounded him, enveloped him, crushed him. A laser beam of pain streaked through his back and neck when the force of it bent him forward, twisting him in a grotesque pose. He reached for the sky, finally screaming the first thing, the only thing, repeating in his panicked mind.

"Help me!"

But snow came down, blotting out the blue sky, and Matt watched as the whiteness fractured into an exploding prism of light. A thousand rainbows burst behind his eyes.

And then . . . darkness.

His breath was whisper thin, ragged in his mouth. He swallowed. *Blood.* His tongue immediately probed the line of teeth to find an empty socket. Upper tooth, behind the canine, but it wasn't in his mouth.

His first thought: *Why can't I see?*

Matt reached to wipe his eyes, but his right arm didn't move. Nothing did. Only his left fist, pressed close to his nose, wiggled. He inhaled again, but it was a half breath, compressed and tight.

Second thought: *It's a horrible dream.* A dream of being buried alive, choking on nothing, gasping like a fish on land.

Third thought: *I'm not dreaming.*

"No!" His scream gurgled, and blood flew out into the small pocket of air around his head. Red flecks splashing onto gray snow.

Fourth thought: *Calm down, calm down, calm down. Don't panic.*

But he did panic. Every muscle contracted, jerking, twisting, fighting.

"Help!" Matt punched the space in front of him, but it was pointless. He had no leverage. He tried twisting his arm, wedging it back and forth against the snow but terrified of what might happen if he freed it. *Would more snow fall down?*

But panic won. Matt heaved back and forth until he gasped, which took all of ten seconds.

Don't use up your air, he thought, relaxing his fists. *Breathe small. Breathe shallow.* How long had it been? A minute? Ten? He wondered how far down he was from the surface.

Matt's fingers curled tightly, touching something hard against his chest.

The beacon.

Matt fumbled against his zipper, and in the few inches of space he had he was able to grab the rope and tug the receiver up to his chin. He didn't even know if it was working, or how to turn it on, but in the darkness a cherry-red light pulsed. *On,* he thought. *It must be on. Carter told me so.* Bending his head down farther, he watched the screen flash.

SE—SE—SE—SE—SE...

He didn't know what it meant—he hadn't been told. But he also hadn't asked. His right arm was still wedged above his head, and his shoulder muscles burned. He squeezed his biceps and triceps, trying to get the blood flowing and the circulation going. He curled his fingers, twisted his wrist. It hurt, but it didn't hurt so much that he suspected anything was broken. He remembered reaching up and wondered if that meant he was facing up. *Or am I upside down?* The thought was too awful to bear; bile rose in his throat.

"Don't puke, don't puke," he mumbled. There was no room to be sick in here. He believed if he was upside down his head would be throbbing. But it wasn't. Not really. He became convinced the light was above him, possibly because the alternative was too awful to contemplate. Maybe there was only a foot of snow above him. *Maybe I can dig my way out.*

He knew he didn't have much time. A glance down showed the beacon still blinking, and he hoped that meant they could find him. He slowed down his pulse, his breath. In the intense silence, a sharp needle of doubt poked his brain.

What if everyone was buried? What if no one's left? What if they were all trapped?

He had to dig. He had to try something. He couldn't wait for help that might never arrive. Patience was not a virtue right now. It was a death sentence.

With his left hand shaking Matt began to dig. One scoop, another, and a scrape. He gasped. *Just keep going,* he thought. *Don't think.*

He retried his locked right arm, commanding himself to bend his elbow. Bend his wrist. Wiggle fingers. "Dammit," he swore. "Shit. Hell. Fuck. Piss." He went through every filthy word he knew, even making up some new ones, then started all over from the beginning. The SE light was still flashing, then made a chirping tweet. He didn't know what that meant and hoped it didn't mean the transmitter had stopped. Another cold slither snaked through his guts—sweat pooled under his chin. Despite all the snow he was hot, sweltering. *It's like trying to dig out of my own grave.*

Flickering spots appeared, fuzzy needles of black on the outside edges of his vision. He pushed his chest against the wall of ice, fighting down a gagging sensation, and rocked back and forth, trying to make a bigger hole, trying to gain a little more space to breathe. He flexed his toes, clenched every muscle, then released, pushing and pulling. *Push*, he thought. *Pull. Push. Pull.* His entire back, from neck to knees, was drenched in sweat. He gained an inch, possibly two. He leaned his head forward and chewed away a chunk of snow and swallowed, still tasting blood.

Another chirp. Same as the last one, but this time he felt it.

It was his phone—nestled down in his pocket. How did it turn back on? He recognized the chirpy birdcall. His mom. She had just left a message.

A sudden sad calm came over him—he wondered what dying would feel like. Would it hurt? Or would he just fade out, lose consciousness, and fall into a permanent sleep? He stopped moving; his breath rattled wetly in his throat. He couldn't think of what more to do. He was too tired;

too tired to push, too tired to make a sound. He pressed his cheek against the snow, relief against his sweaty skin. It was so nice and cold. And he was so tired. . . .

Pictures reeled through his head, blobs of light taking shape. A backyard swing set, his red tennis shoes and striped socks. He watched himself swing back and forth, making a thin squeal as the chains pulled. He felt the wind through his hair, the sway and tug on his arms and legs, pressure ebbing and flowing as he tried to defy gravity. Up and down. Back and forth. *Squeak, squeak.* The sound shifted, fell lower, turned into a drone, a jabbering hum, muffled but growing. The white noise broke apart, becoming words. A voice. He understood it. "Here!" It yelled. "Here! I found him!" He opened his eyes; someone was shouting his name. He wanted to yell back, but his tongue was as heavy as a sack of sand in his mouth. He couldn't seem to get the words out.

"Matt! Matt! Hang on!"

When he blinked again everything was brighter. Louder. Light brought noise, more shouting and grunting and scraping sounds.

"This way! Like this! Careful with that shovel!"

A spiderweb of sunshine cracked through, and with it came air, inflating his lungs.

"He's alive!" Shadows moved over him. "He's conscious!"

Another voice bleated, "But where's Dylan?"

"Keep shoveling! Don't stop!" Matt recognized Carter's

voice as the snow moved away, revealing his face, then shoulders and torso. His arm was free.

"Matt! Hang on! We'll get you out!" Carter dug like a terrier, like a person possessed. "Is anything broken?"

"I . . ." Matt's voice cracked. "I don't think so." His legs were still stuck fast, so he pushed his arms against the pile, moving the snow away, feeling like one of those giant sea turtles flailing their flippers as they dug a hole in the sand. When he got down to his thighs he was able to finally break free, one knee, then the second popping up like he was bursting through rubble. His skis were nowhere to be found, but he still had both poles looped around his wrists.

"Oh man, are you lucky!" Carter exhaled and rolled back on his butt with a thud. He held up his beacon. "Looks like these things work."

"Where's Tony?" Matt asked, panting. "Where's Sid?"

"Tony's fine." Carter tucked his beacon back into his coat. "He was above me when the snow pack broke." He examined the small shovel in his hands, then stabbed it down next to him. "I knew that slab looked wrong."

Matt tried to stand but his legs felt like water. He was too shaky to trust them yet. "Where's Sid?"

"Leah's looking." Carter wiped his eyes with the back of his glove, looked over at Julie, who stared blindly at the wide expanse of field, now littered with chunks of ice so big they resembled boulders. She was crying.

"He was a good hundred yards ahead of me," Matt said,

remembering how he'd been trying to catch him. "Dylan was to my left. I ended up veering right into the trees."

"Leah saw you go down," Carter said. "But we still have no idea about Dylan." He dropped his voice. "We can't find him without a beacon."

The beacon. The one Dylan gave him—the one he handed over with a nod and a smile and without a second thought. The one that just saved Matt's life. "Oh." Vomit built suddenly in his throat and he had to roll over onto his stomach to swallow it down.

"It's not your fault, Matt." Carter grabbed his shoulder, but Matt didn't answer. He knew from Carter's voice that he didn't blame him. Carter blamed himself. He was the one on the slab when it broke. "Dylan was in the middle and he got hit by the full slide. Hard." Carter swallowed loudly. "I don't think a beacon would have made a difference."

Matt nodded, unable to disagree. He wanted to believe Carter, but they would never know.

"You were on the edge of it," Carter continued. "It clipped you and you were buried under two feet. That was a huge slide. Probably fifteen feet in the middle."

When Matt turned to look at him, Carter's eyes were huge and wet, bright grass green. Matt didn't really understand what he meant. He shook his head, staring at Carter's eyes, realizing that they weren't deep dark brown like Leah's.

"It would be like having a building fall on you," Carter

said finally, blinking away tears. "She knows that too." He glanced at Julie, who was holding tight to a tree trunk, head bent, still crying. Her shoulders shuddered up and down with her sobs, the only movement in an otherwise stationary landscape.

Matt struggled to his feet, amazed nothing really hurt when he moved, only a few sharp twinges of heat in his neck and lower back. Carter gaped at him, disbelieving. "I guess you're tougher than you look."

"I don't feel very tough." He watched Julie, unsure of what to do, what to say. He thought they should look for Dylan, but when he examined the aftermath of the avalanche, he realized trying to find him would be almost exactly like looking for a needle in a haystack. "If you hadn't found me when you did . . ." He turned away. He couldn't think about Dylan right now. He had to believe Carter—that there was no hope, there was nothing they could do about it now. He had to believe it or he really would be sick. "We need to find Sid." Matt propped himself up, and using his poles for support, forced himself into a forward lurch down the hill.

Sid's beacon worked—Leah and Tony found him within minutes, made easier by the fact that he wasn't completely buried in snow as Matt had been. Sid's head and shoulders were free, but from what Matt could tell it looked like the force of the slide had knocked him directly into a huge timber, pinning him against it like a bug.

He was unconscious when they found him—moaning by the time Carter, Julie, and Matt finally arrived at the base of the run.

"Carter!" Leah barked, ignoring the rest of them. "I need you!"

Like brother, like sister, Matt thought as he watched Leah shoveling snow as if it was the tryouts for the shoveling Olympics and there was only one spot left on the team.

"We need a doctor!" she yelled at him.

"I'm not a doctor!" Carter ran over anyway.

"You're premed, right?" Leah quickly but carefully moved the snow away from Sid, alternating between using her shovel and her hands. Tony cleared snow from the other side.

"That doesn't mean anything," Carter argued.

"We need a stretcher." Matt leaned heavily against a tree. The hike down the hill had just caught up to him—he was sweating again, and the pack he wore felt like it weighed a hundred pounds. Sid's face was the color of ash. *Not good.* Even if nothing was broken, Matt doubted Sid would be able to walk.

No one spoke. Only the sound of digging and heavy breathing and Julie's crying. A part of Matt wanted to shake her, slap her into silence.

Immediately, his face burned. He knew she just lost someone, someone important, someone she might have loved. Matt had never been in love. He didn't know what it felt like, what it looked like, and if it looked like anything, the image Matt had in his head was the way Carter's face looked at Julie's when he had drunkenly interrupted them in the hallway last night. *Naked* was the word that had popped into Matt's mind. Carter's face had looked purely naked, blazing with passion. And if Matt was being honest with himself, he knew he'd never had that feeling before. He certainly had never seen his parents look at each other like that, and then wondered if they ever had. Maybe once, a long time ago. Had Julie been in love with Dylan? With Carter? With them both? Matt dropped his head, turned, and leaned against an aspen trunk and closed his eyes. Who the hell was he to tell Julie how to feel, how to be?

Still, he couldn't stand the sound of her whimpers, as if she was in physical pain. "Here . . ." He came up behind her, hands opened up. "Julie? Can you help me find some big branches?"

She blinked at him, shaking her head as if not understanding his meaning. Her face and eyelids were swollen, cheeks stained where mascara left inky streaks. Snot glistened on her upper lip.

"C'mon," he tried again, touching her shoulder. "Sid needs our help now."

The look she returned—pure hatred. Or was it pain? Matt couldn't tell. She looked as if she just got her hand slammed in a door and it was all his fault. "What did you say?" Her eyes were enormous, black pupils swallowing up violet irises.

Is she in shock? Matt had heard that people can just lose it, or they disappear into themselves without a sound, becoming vacant. But he'd never seen it. And he didn't know what to do to stop it. She wasn't freaking out, not yet, but he could see in her face how it would go if he said the wrong thing.

"We need to make a stretcher," he repeated, slower this time. It was important to stay calm, stay logical. "Or something Sid can lie on so we can carry him."

"Stretcher," she said dully, wiping her face with her glove.

"Yes." Matt saw that Tony and Leah's digging had Sid almost free, and Carter was asking him questions.

"Can you move your arms? Your legs? Your head? Your neck?"

"My left leg," Sid gasped, his face bleached of color. He inhaled deeply and started coughing. "My chest," he said after his hacking fit subsided. "It really hurts to breathe."

Carter unzipped Sid's coat, lifted his shirt, and from Matt's position he could only see Carter's and Leah's faces as they examined him. Their expressions didn't look reassuring.

"Do we have a first aid kit?" Matt asked Julie, but she didn't answer. Her eyes had the flat effect of a blind person. She stared straight ahead without seeing him.

"First aid kit won't help," Carter said. "It's internal, I think."

"What do you mean?" Matt forced himself to walk

over and look, prepared for something ghastly—blood, guts, bone fragments protruding. Something gory and irreparable.

In the middle of Sid's chest a dark splotch, like a giant purple island, extended from the right shoulder down to underneath his rib cage. If anything, it looked like a really big, really painful bruise.

"Definitely a hematoma," Carter told Leah.

"Hema what?" Tony asked. He held his brother's wrist in his hand, monitoring his pulse. Tony was breathing fast himself, without a rhythm, and Matt knew Tony only ever did that when he got really upset. The last time Matt had seen Tony look like that was when he got a C- on a physics exam—a combination of sheer bewilderment and sudden terror.

"Bruise," Leah said.

"Probably cracked ribs. Pneumothorax. I can't really tell."

Leah didn't answer. She looked away as if she already knew the answer.

"What's a pneumo . . . ?" Tony looked like he was going to scream. He inhaled sharply. "English please!"

"It means a collapsed lung," Leah told him, and Matt wondered how she knew that.

"Okay," Tony held a hand to his face, covering his eyes, "so what do we do?"

"We need to get him out of here. He needs a hospital."

"How much time?" Leah asked Carter.

"Time?" Tony jumped up. "Time for what?" Frantic, he pulled out his phone. "We need to call nine-one-one!" He spun around, moving in circles, a nonsensical dance between the trees. "I can't get a signal!"

Matt had the sudden urge to knock him down, a need to restrain him somehow. Tony twirled around like a top, trying to get his phone to work. He looked like he was swatting away an imaginary swarm of flies, and the more Matt watched, the more he felt the panic swim inside him. His vision blurred. His knees quivered. Did he have injuries of his own—something not immediately apparent? He took a breath and checked his own phone, surprised to find it wasn't broken, but the battery was on its last bar. Here, down at the base of the run in the heavy cover of trees, the signal was nonexistent. "I can't get one either."

"All right," Carter said, checking his own with the same result. "Does anyone have a working phone?"

Leah bit her lip. "I didn't bring mine."

"What?"

"It was already low so I left it in Dylan's car, in the charger."

"Shit." Carter exhaled. His eyes landed on Julie. "What about you, Jules?"

"Dylan had my phone and some of my stuff in his waterproof sack," she answered, then convulsed into a fresh round of tears at the mention of his name.

"Sid? Sid?" Tony squeezed his brother's shoulders, patted his cheek, but Sid had passed out. His breathing was wet and thick. Tony fumbled in Sid's pack, finally retrieving the shattered phone, cradling it in his palms as if it was a dead baby bird. "Oh no."

"So we have three phones," Leah said. "All low on juice."

"Mine's fine," argued Carter.

"Yeah, but it's useless if we can't get a signal," Leah told him. "We need to get out of here."

"I know." Carter grimaced. "But I don't want to move him."

"We have to."

"Maybe we can get him to the cabin." Matt suddenly remembered their destination point. He turned to the left, wondering if that was north or east. "Dylan said we were less than a mile away. Maybe there'll be something there. Maybe there'll be a first aid kit or a radio or . . . something."

"You think?" Tony was hopeful.

"There could be some emergency supplies. Blankets. Something we can use. Maybe the phones will work there. We can't stay here." The sunlight had faded—afternoon was gone and the shadows grew longer on the snow. "And we need to go if we want to find it before dark."

"I have a two-person tent," Carter said, and Matt realized how much Carter really didn't want to move Sid.

"Cabin's better," Matt said quickly, giving an anxious glance at Julie. "Better shelter. We should at least try to find it."

"Okay. You're right." Carter popped off his skis and handed them over to Matt, whose skis remained buried somewhere up on the ridge. "You, Julie, and Leah try to tamp down a track for us," he explained. "Tony and I will wear the snowshoes. That should help."

"What?" Julie wiped her face. "You mean we're just going to leave? Without Dylan?" Her voice was thin and high, dangerously close to breaking. "We have to keep looking!"

"Julie, I know." Carter threw up his hands. "I did look. We all looked. We could be out there all night looking. It's too late. . . ."

"It's not!" Julie screamed. "It's not too late!"

"Julie," Leah tried, "it's been over an hour. It's a miracle that we found Matt, and he had the beacon."

Matt's face went so hot at that fact, he had to look away. He couldn't meet Julie's eyes. He couldn't even swallow his spit.

"It's also a miracle that Sid's still alive," Carter said. "And he won't stay that way unless we get help."

Tony's face went as pale as his brother's, and for a moment Matt thought his best friend was going to faint. Tony wobbled back, considering Carter's diagnosis, and then sat down with a plop.

Julie kicked the snow with her boot, punched the side of the tree, then grabbed her skis and started off between the trees without another word. Her face was a mask of nothing, but her eyes said otherwise.

"Good," Leah said quietly, more to herself. "All right, let's go."

"Do you know where you're going?" Leah asked Matt. Matt was skiing somewhat haphazardly. Right then left, then stopping and starting, turning around to check on Tony and Carter's progress with Sid, which was slow and plodding but steady.

"No. Not really." He tried not to show his exhaustion, but his head was pounding again. He needed to find the cabin. After all, it had been his idea. He was certain they were headed in the right direction, but then again, the landscape had a uniformity to it that was disconcerting. Every tree and ridgeline looked exactly like the next. The sun had set—his clue they were going west, but soon he would have no light to guide them.

"Did he say it was west?" Leah asked, not ready to say Dylan's name. For now, Julie was quiet, skiing calmly behind them.

"Yeah." Matt looked back. Carter and Tony were about twenty yards back, Sid lolling between them in a basket carry, keeping up thanks to the snowshoes. The snow was not as deep here, but in some places the drifts went over Matt's knees. "Maybe I should help carry."

"No." Leah watched the darkening sky. "We need to keep moving. There's only about a half hour of light left." She glided forward, peering between the trees. "He better have been right about this place," she added under her breath.

Like a spell being cast with her last word, the cabin finally came into view. At first it looked like another boulder or a fallen tree—dark, squat, and small—with a stacked stone chimney on the far side. The roof, mostly covered in fresh snow, sloped deeply like a Swiss chalet, reminding Matt of something from a fairy tale. *The place where a witch lives.*

"That has to be it!" Tony exclaimed as they staggered up behind them. "Thank God!"

"There's a chimney," Carter gasped, somewhat happily. "That means we can build a fire and maybe send up a signal!"

Matt puffed a breath of relief, knowing he did something right. He pushed forward on his poles, skiing so fast he almost ran right into the front door. He jabbed it with his pole, but the wood slab was swollen with dampness. It didn't budge. He clicked out of his skis as Leah arrived. "Open?"

"If not, I'm going to make it." He jammed his shoulder against the door and it popped open, swinging into gray darkness. Against the far wall he saw a chair sitting underneath the one small paned window. He clopped in, floor squeaking and shuddering under his weight. It smelled of dry rot, pine, and something musty. *Probably rodent.* Matt unfolded a metal cot with squeaky protest. It was an old army cot—a double—with a sleeping bag rolled on top. "This will make a decent bed for Sid," he mumbled, sitting down to see if it would hold.

"Are there any matches?" Leah held up an old lantern. "I think this has an unused oil canister in it."

"I hope so." The fireplace was an empty black mouth, devoid of wood. "Then at least we can build a fire." It wasn't cold in the cabin, but it was damp. Matt knew the temperature would drop fast during the night.

Julie walked in, stared at the floor, the ceiling, then a large metal chest behind the chair. Like the cot, it appeared to be military supply, an old army-issue foot-locker. "What's in there?"

"Well, it's not locked," Leah said, snapping up the brass latches. It opened with a tinny creak. "Blanket. Matches. Candles. Soda." She named each item as she removed it and set it carefully on the floor. "Tarp. National Geographic magazine. Flashlight. Batteries . . ."

"Batteries?" Tony asked from the doorway. He leaned heavily against it, catching his breath. "What kind?"

"Double D," Leah answered. "Just for the flashlight."

"Oh." Tony shrugged, obviously hoping for a different kind. "Matt? Can you help us?"

"Of course." Matt stood up, embarrassed to be caught resting, and the pounding in his head restarted its angry beat. "I think this cot will work for Sid."

"Good. He needs to lie down." Tony wiped his forehead. "So do I."

Between the three of them it was easy to lift and move Sid. He let out a small groan as they shifted him onto the cot. His eyelids fluttered but didn't open. "Water," he whispered.

"Okay brother," Tony said softly. "Hang on. I'll get you water." He put his hand gently on Sid's forehead as if he were a small, helpless creature. It reminded Matt why Tony was his best friend, though he knew he wasn't Tony's. Tony's admiration for his older brother was obvious, even if he never said so, and Matt thought again how nice it would have been to have had a brother growing up, or just another sibling—someone else who was on his team. Small, hot needles prickled in his throat. He'd always wanted that, wished for it, prayed for it. How did that line go? *Be careful what you wish for, you might just get it.* He wasn't sure who had said that one—it hadn't been in his quote book. Shaking his head, Matt pulled his sweatshirt out of his backpack and rolled it into a pillow. Carefully, he lifted Sid's head, slipped it under him, and gingerly lay him back.

"More upright," Carter insisted. "I think he should be elevated more."

Tony balled up the matching pair of sweatpants. Then he emptied Sid's pack to use as many pieces of clothing required to get the angle right, before going outside to fill his brother's water bottle with fresh snow.

"Is that comfortable?" Carter asked Sid.

Sid nodded, eyelids fluttering. "Better."

"Good."

"Should we build a fire?" Matt wondered aloud. "Maybe the smoke will send up a signal."

"Can't hurt, I guess," Carter replied. "But it's almost dark now, so no one will see it."

"Oh."

"Won't matter if they do see it," Leah said, putting everything back in the footlocker. "No one's looking for us."

"Won't they come looking?" Matt asked her, confused. "At least by tomorrow?"

"Doubt it."

"Won't they notice we didn't sign out? Plus, the cars are still in the lot."

Leah slammed the footlocker lid shut. She took a deep breath. "Dylan didn't sign us in."

"What?" Carter asked, stunned. "What did you say?"

"I heard him tell Julie," Leah said slowly, watching Julie, who was sitting cross-legged in front of the small stone fireplace, staring blankly at the hearth. "Said he didn't want anyone to know about this place, so he didn't write down where we were going."

"Oh. My. God." Carter sank to his knees like someone had just punched him. "Julie! What the hell? Is this true?"

"Is what true?" Tony reappeared with the water bottle.

Julie didn't answer. Instead she rocked back and forth like a stubborn toddler who refused to listen. She even put her hands over her ears.

"What the fu . . ." Carter didn't finish. His head collapsed into his hands as if he couldn't bear to have anyone see his face.

An icy churn stirred Matt's stomach, and the floor seemed to shift under his feet. "But the cars," he insisted. "Someone will see the cars and call it in, right?"

Carter looked up and nodded. "Yeah, I hope so. But it could be days before they'll find us out here." He glanced at his sister, then Sid. Matt suddenly understood Carter's real distress.

Sid wouldn't live that long.

"We'll just go back to get help," Matt said.

Carter shook his head. "Someone needs to stay here."

"I'll stay with him." Tony shook the water bottle until the snow resembled wet slush.

"I need to stay too," Carter said. "If I'm the only one with first aid training."

"Then I'll go back myself," Matt volunteered without thinking. He didn't have to. It wasn't even something to think about, it was just something that needed to be done.

"Matt . . ."

"Someone has to go. I can do ten miles."

"Not right now you can't," Carter said. "You're exhausted. You're practically falling down. Plus, it's dark out. You'll get lost."

"I'll go with him," Leah drew her knees up and wrapped her arms around herself. "I know how to get back."

"I know you know," Carter said, frustrated. "But I don't want you going out there now."

"I can handle it."

"I know that too." Carter raked his hands through his

hair, as if there were another option he hadn't thought of.

"Do you have a map or something?" Tony wanted to know. He gave Sid small sips from the water bottle.

"Don't need one," Leah replied. "I know how to get back." Her words had a calm intensity, coupled with a hardness that made Matt believe her.

"Wait, wait." Carter waved his hands. "Let's just slow down here. Let's think about this."

"There's not much to think about," Leah answered. "The phones don't work here and there is no radio."

"I know, but . . ."

"Carter," Julie sat up and stopped rocking back and forth. "Leah's right. We need to go back."

"Julie." Carter sighed her name. "Someone has to stay with Sid."

"Tony will," Julie replied, nodding at Tony. "Of course he'll stay."

"I'm not leaving them on their own," Carter argued. "Plus, you're in no condition to leave either."

"I'm fine."

"You're not fine."

"Okay." Julie put her head back down on her knees. "I'm not fine. But that doesn't change the facts."

"I know," Carter sighed. He crossed his arms and turned back to the dark cave of the fireplace. "Okay, I'll stay here with Sid and Tony. I want you to stay with me, Julie." He turned around and dropped his arms. "That's what I want," he repeated. To Matt it almost sounded like he was begging.

Julie didn't answer at first. "I'll stay, then."

Carter nodded and quickly wiped his eyes. He turned to Matt. "Leah will go with you," he said. "She'll lead you out."

"It's okay," Matt said, wondering why Carter thought his little sister could handle the trek if he couldn't. "I don't need—"

"Leah goes with!" Carter was firm, on the edge of a shout. "No one's going out there alone."

"Okay," Matt agreed. "When do we leave?" Outside the dirty window it was past dusk, shadows blurring into one another.

"Right now."

"Now? It's almost pitch black out there!" Tony exclaimed.

"Then we'll need this." Leah clicked on the flashlight, making a moonbeam on the ceiling, and tossed it over to Carter. "Pack us light. We need to go fast. We need a good phone."

Shockingly, Matt's phone was deemed the best, with slightly more battery power than Carter's. Tony's phone hadn't even gotten a signal up on the last ridge. Carter took Leah's backpack, emptying out anything extraneous, before adding a few things from his own pack. Matt wondered how he could decide what was necessary and what wasn't. Right now it seemed all the bare essentials they had weren't nearly enough.

Leah struck a match, lit the oil canister in the lantern

as easily as if she'd done it a hundred times before, then set it on the footlocker. A wavering golden glow illuminated the cobwebs in the corners.

"So what should *we* do?" Tony asked.

Leah watched the light move like waves across the ceiling. "Build a signal fire."

Tony stared at his brother. "And then what?"

"I don't know." Leah shrugged her shoulders, then readjusted her hat, tucking her curls underneath as she gave him a sad smile. "Pray, I guess." She nodded to Matt. "You ready?"

"Yeah, I am," he said, not having the heart to tell her that Tony was an atheist. "Bunch of bunkum," he liked to tell Matt whenever the subject came up, and Matt would always agree. He wondered if Tony would pray now. *Yes,* Matt decided, *he would.* Tony would pray to God, Jesus, Allah, Loki, Kali, Buddha, Odin, Santa Claus, and the Easter bunny if he thought it would help his brother. Tony would pray to Obi-Wan Kenobi and try to use the Force. And Matt knew he would do the same. "I'm ready when you are."

Ten minutes later they started out, skiing fast in the moonlight, backtracking over the trail with such intensity that Matt felt the now-familiar sensation of building nausea. He couldn't keep going at this pace, but ahead of him Leah showed no signs of slowing. "Hold up!" he finally shouted, his voice frighteningly loud in the still woods.

"Sorry." Leah pulled to a stop. "I know. I'm exhausted too, but it's bad, Matt."

"You mean Sid, don't you?"

"Yeah." She leaned over her poles, taking big breaths. "We need to get a call out before morning. They won't send out rescue until first light and they need to know where to find them."

"What's going to happen to Sid?" Matt knew she had an inkling of how serious it was. He sensed she had been holding back, maybe to prevent Tony from panicking.

"His lung is probably collapsed," she said quietly. "And who knows what other internal injuries he has from hitting that tree. If he doesn't get to a hospital, he could suffocate to death."

"So what is the plan?" Matt tried to keep his voice calm. Immediately he remembered what it felt like to slowly lose air, to have to fight for every breath. And now that was happening to Sid. He squeezed his poles in a vise grip, forcing the memory from his head.

"We get up on a ridge and make the call. And if that doesn't work we'll head back to Berthoud Pass and find help." Leah pointed off into the darkness, although the combination of moonlight and snow made everything quite bright. Even though Matt couldn't see the mountains, he could feel them looming ahead in the distance. "I remember the coordinates of the cabin, so don't turn on your phone until we get up there."

"Got it."

They continued on, making no sound except for the swish of skis through powder. Matt concentrated on Leah's back and her smooth stride that he did his best to match. She went on like a machine, never flagging. He was both frustrated and awed by her robotic determination.

"We need to get to the top before midnight," she said.

"Why?" He did a quick mental calculation, assuming it was past nine. That meant three more hours of skiing, which mostly meant hiking up a mountain, and the way she said it implied they wouldn't be stopping if they wanted to make it on time. Defeat simmered through his bones like an ache. It sounded impossible.

"Storm might be blowing in early," she puffed. "We'll need to be off the summit if it does."

Matt glanced up at the navy sky, bright with moonlight, completely cloudless. "It's so nice out." It *was* nice. Not too cold and barely a breeze. It was another reminder that despite their desperate situation, things could be a lot worse.

"That was yesterday. Yesterday was clear."

She didn't have to elaborate—his brain filled in the rest.

Yesterday was clear and look what happened.

"Just let me know what you need me to do and I'll do it," Matt said, suddenly thankful she was with him. He didn't know too much about survival in the wilderness, nor did he have any practical experience. All his knowledge up until this point had come from books—books his father had given him and told him to read. Like his *Ultimate Book of Famous Quotations*. "Useful for any situation," his father had said when Matt unwrapped the present. It was an early twelfth birthday present, and the last thing his father gave him before moving out of their house the following week. True to his father's word, he thought of a quote from the book. "Energy and persistence conquer all things."

"Nice," Leah replied. "So who said that?"

"Benjamin Franklin."

"Did Benjamin Franklin ever climb a mountain?"

"Don't think so."

"Yeah, that's what I thought." Leah turned away and began the long, slow ascent. Up and up and forever up.

THE HUNTER
Location: Avalanche site,
Two miles north from cabin

The night air was still soft. Warm and wet. The cat stood still, watching the moonlight shift over the ground and the expanse of snow. No movement, no sound. The trail had been easy to follow all morning, but here the scent vanished. Something had changed.

The cat sniffed deeply, tasting the air. It didn't like the look of the field; it *smelled* wrong. The ground here was bad. Not solid. And the cat would not cross it. Instead, it turned back, going around through the trees, finding a different way, and after a few minutes a new smell twitched its nose.

With a flick of its tail the cat trotted on, hunger moving it forward.

TONY

Location: Abandoned NFS cabin,
Arapaho National Forest
Elevation: 9,000 feet

"Try to find dry pieces," Carter told Tony. "Dead stuff. As much as you can carry."

"Got it." Tony peered into the growing dark. Thankfully, the moon was full, easy enough to see by, and he headed for a wall of thick fir trees twenty yards up the slope from the cabin. As he trudged uphill, he noticed how the cabin was situated almost like a pebble in the bottom of a giant bowl, and he plowed through the knee-high drifts with steady persistence. Halfway up, he pulled out his phone, turned his back to the trees, and held it up. The battery was still at half, but the signal was nonexistent. Carter had said something about the mountain interference, and while Tony didn't doubt him, he was the type of person who always needed to test things for himself. No matter what he'd been told.

But in this case Carter was correct. "Shit," Tony muttered and slid the phone back into his front pocket, careful to zip it shut. He certainly wasn't going to be the idiot who lost his phone in a snowbank, even if it didn't work. Still grumbling, he headed back up to the trees, realizing the ultimate irony was that when you really were depending on technology to rescue you, you only learned of its limitations.

Tony pushed away a snow-covered limb, wondering how he would find anything dry under so much frozen water. With a grunt he scooted under the branches, and once underneath realized he could barely see his hand in front of his face. "Dammit." He waited a few seconds for his eyes to adjust, and when they did he noticed that underneath the branches there was a wide open space, big as a tent and nearly tall enough to stand up in. Upon closer inspection he noticed dull-looking stubs jutting out from the main trunk, and to Tony's relief they broke off easily in his grip, like stale crackers. Dead wood. Exactly what he needed. He quickly removed every available stub and stick until he had a whole armful. He even stuffed some withered-looking pinecones into his coat, and as he turned to exit the tree shelter, he heard something that froze him still.

A low growl. A curdling rumble. Tony held his breath. A sigh. An exhalation of breath. His? No. Not his. He counted his pulse and when it hit thirty beats he backed out from underneath the branches, muscles tight, eyes darting over the bright open sheet of snow.

Nothing moved. Nothing there. No sound. No wind.

"Carter?"

Silence.

He watched the cabin. The dull glow from the lantern was visible, and the place reminded Tony of a small island surrounded by a giant white sea. He blinked again, feeling that peculiar sensation shiver his scalp, tightening the skin under his hair. The sensation of being watched.

"Carter?"

"Yeah?"

Tony jumped. Carter was right there, standing a few yards down the hill, off to the left with his own armload of sticks.

"Oh," Tony said, feeling disoriented. "Nothing." He had been sure Carter had been behind him. That's where the noise had been. Or had it? Tony pivoted around, wondering if now his mind was playing tricks on him. The woods were still. Nothing there. *Must have been a bird,* Tony thought, feeling stupid and relieved at the same time. "I found a bunch of dead sticks and some pinecones."

"Good." Carter turned and tromped back down the hill to the cabin. "Let's go make ourselves a fire."

Tony hurried after him, forcing himself not to look back.

MATT

Location: Byers Peak
Elevation: 12,804 feet

The last hundred yards weren't the hardest, but to Matt they felt like the longest. At this elevation the wind was strong, freezing the sweat on the back of his neck as he gingerly picked his way along the narrow track until he reached Leah resting on a wide expanse of granite. She was perched on a section about twenty feet square. On either side the slope fell away into the air and a hundred-foot drop to whatever happened to be below. Matt didn't know, and he certainly wasn't about to look. He felt dizzy and lightheaded just imagining it.

"You made it." Leah sat cross-legged on the rock like a yogi.

"How high are we?" Matt gasped. Every breath he gulped seemed to contain the absolute bare minimum of oxygen to prevent losing consciousness. It felt as though his ribs had turned into steel bands around his chest, slowly compressing so that every breath seemed smaller and more useless than the last.

"Definitely over twelve thousand feet."

"So *where* are we?" He sat down as gracefully as he could, managed to unclip his boots, and carefully stacked his skis on the rock. He didn't want to do something stupid and have them go sailing off into the abyss.

"Byers Peak, I think," Leah turned her head, orienting herself. "To the south is Bills Peak. North is Morse Mountain." She squinted into the distance, her diamond stud flashing in the moonlight like a beacon. "Over there is Sheep Mountain—I think that's what it's called."

Great, Matt thought. *Everything is mountains.*

"Highway 40 is east." Matt followed her direction, for some reason expecting to see it. But there was nothing but a gauzy whiteness, rolling out into dark sky.

With a mumble on his breath that sounded like a prayer, Matt pulled out his phone and turned it on. Low battery but Leah was right, the signal was strong. Matt grinned, relieved. "It works!" One message was waiting—the message his dad had sent. "Who should I call first?"

"Nine-one-one."

"Right." *Idiot.* He punched in the numbers, the wind whipping and getting stronger. Little flecks of sleet stung his cheek.

He heard a buzz, a click as the signal went through, and after two beats the operator answered.

"Nine-one-one—what is your emergency?"

"Hello!" Matt yelled, embarrassed, nervous, and excited in a way that suggested he was doing something illegal. He'd never called 911 before. His throat felt weird. His neck hair stood up. He couldn't hear very well; he took off his ski helmet and pressed the receiver tight against his ear. "Hello! My name is Matt! I'm out at Berthoud Pass ski area! There was an avalanche. One missing!" He didn't say dead. "One injured! Bad! We need someone to fly in! Um . . ." He was babbling—words coming out of his mouth so fast and so loud, wondering if the operator could hear him above the wind.

"Where are you exactly? Please repeat and slow down. One injury?"

"Berthoud Pass," he repeated, realizing that was incorrect. "I mean, right now I'm on Byers Peak, I think."

"Berthoud Pass? How many are in your party?"

"Yes. No. I mean, uh seven of us." *Now six.* "One severe injury!"

A buzz on the line. Static.

"Matt!" Leah jumped up from the rock, looking like she wanted to punch him. "Give them the coordinates of the cabin!"

"Not Berthoud Pass!" He yelled into the phone, but his yell was ripped away in the wind. A sharp gust pushed him sideways and he had to squat down to keep his balance. "I have coordinates! Thirty-nine! Fifty-one! Forty-four! One hundred and five! Fifty-three! Twenty-nine!" He read the numbers off the scrap of paper Leah shoved in front of him, but the numbers were scribbly, and the moonlight had vanished in the increasing clouds.

"Not Berthoud Pass? Please repeat."

"No!" He screamed, lurching away from Leah in an angry panic. The numbers. He had to remember the numbers, and he squeezed his eyes shut with the effort. He slowed down as each one returned to his mind, morphing out of the ether like a developing photograph. Those were the right numbers. "Listen to me! Thirty-nine degrees, fifty-one minutes, forty-four seconds north! One hundred and five degrees, fifty-three minutes, and twenty-nine seconds west! Those are coordinates!" he bellowed. "I repeat! Those are coordinates for survivors! One injured badly!"

"Okay. Slow down."

The crackling fuzz vanished. Matt spun around, aghast, wondering if the phone had just died, but no, the battery was still there. He'd just lost the signal. "I can try again!" he hollered. "I just got cut off!"

"Matt?"

He turned around at the fear in Leah's voice, holding his phone like it was a bomb. "What's wrong?"

"Don't!" Leah yelled above the howling wind. "Don't move."

"I . . ."

"Matt! Don't . . ." Leah's words were interrupted by a weird crunch, like the muffled sound of glass breaking. And as Matt looked around, he saw he was no longer on the rock. In his need to get his message through he had walked out onto the snow pack, which turned out to be a dissolving sheet of ice.

Another crack. *Oh shit,* he thought weakly. One second later his boots went out from under him as the ice sheet gave way. *Pop-pop-pop-pop . . .* It sounded like firecrackers going off.

He slid, picking up speed as he headed for the center of the gully—a giant trough of glare ice.

"Dig in!" Leah screamed, but her voice was already starting to fade out of hearing.

Dig into what? He flipped over onto his stomach but skittered so fast that momentum kept him going, landing him back on his shoulders, faceup, the back of his head clunking heavily on the ice. But he didn't feel it—every part of him was hitting something as he bounced down the field.

His arms flailed in a seizurelike fit and his helmet went flying, bouncing out of his grip. He jammed his boot heels into the ice sheet, but the nylon on his pants and jacket had no friction. He didn't slow down. His boots scudded and scraped, grit flew up in his face; he was no match for the steep slope. *Gravity sucks.* Matt tried again, picking up his feet and slamming them back. Golf ball–size chunks of dirty ice splintered off in small explosions. He knew he needed to get in control, find a way to slow down, find a way to stop himself. A second later, his right leg collided with a protruding rock, sending a shockwave of pain up his ankle, kneecap combusting into excruciating spasms.

He spun left, using every muscle that remained to raise his head off the ice, knowing that if he'd hit it on that boulder he'd already be a goner.

Still, he didn't stop. If anything, he was going faster. Using his elbows, he propped himself up almost to sitting, but then what he saw made him want to fall back down.

Nothing.

The edge.

Open air.

And he was headed right for it.

TONY

Location: Abandoned NFS cabin,
Arapaho National Forest
Elevation: 9,000 feet

"I should have gone with them." Julie stared at the pile of kindling and logs that Tony had arranged in the hearth. "I should go back and look for Dylan. We shouldn't have left him like that."

All Tony could think was, *Left him like what exactly? Dead?* He bit his lip and squashed a few more old pinecones under the twigs.

"Julie." Carter sighed, rubbing his eyes. "I know, I know. But Leah will do it. She'll get a signal out. Believe me. And once they know where we are, they'll send out a rescue at dawn. We just have to sit tight, okay?"

"You don't know that," she replied dully, chin in her hands.

"I know my sister." Carter wadded up sections of the old National Geographic magazine into tight bundles. There was not much paper, but if the kindling caught it would get hot enough to start the old wood.

Tony noticed that neither of them had mentioned Matt, either because they had no confidence in his abilities or they had already forgotten his existence. "Matt's tough," he told Julie. "He'll make it."

"Dylan was tough." Julie stared back at him as though he'd just said something particularly disgusting. Her upper lip curled. "And he was smart. But he didn't make it, did he?"

Tony had the urge to ask her how smart Dylan really was if he didn't wear an avalanche beacon, but he also realized that was the only reason Matt survived, and he certainly didn't want to remind her of that. He bit down on his lip even harder and continued stacking twigs in a neat teepee around the logs. "Okay," he said, ignoring Julie. "Carter, I think this looks pretty good."

A gurgling cough from his brother made Tony drop his stick. "Sid?" The light in the cabin was dim—only the lantern flickering, distorting the size and shape of things, including Sid's face, which was now twisted with pain. His eyes popped open like a puppet's as he struggled for breath.

"Sid!" Tony put a hand to his brother's forehead, unsure where to touch him, wondering if he should at all. "Where does it hurt?"

"Everywhere," Sid wheezed, straining forward. Carter leaned over them, holding the lantern, a frustrated helplessness turning his mouth into a flat line. "Every time I breathe it feels like I'm being stabbed."

"Dammit." Carter swung the light around the room like a sea captain on a ship, peering into the darkness looking for clues. He checked his watch. "They've only been gone two hours."

"And?" Tony wiped the sweat from Sid's forehead with his shirt sleeve.

"*And* I don't know." Carter tromped the perimeter of the cabin, searching for something useful, something he might have missed. "Even if I did, we don't have anything here to help us. Not even a radio." He kicked the side of the footlocker.

Carter was growing frustrated, and the last thing Tony wanted was another person losing it. He needed Carter to stay calm. He needed Carter, period. "Maybe we should open the window," Tony suggested. "And open the door. Let in some fresh air."

"No," Julie said from her lump in the corner. "It's too cold out there."

"Well, it's stuffy as hell in here," Carter replied, a bit too sharply. To make his point, to make it clear to Julie he was in charge, he wedged open the small window, forcing it against the swollen sash until it finally swung free, shattering one of the panes as a result.

"Nice," Julie whispered, but it sounded more like a sneer. Tony flinched, knowing he needed to say something, say the right thing. *That's always been Matt's area,* he thought desperately. *Matt always knew what to say.* But Matt wasn't here.

"Please don't." Carter swung the window back and forth, creating a breeze. The rusted hinges squawked in protest. "Please don't."

"Don't what?" Julie asked, effectively starting *it*.

Carter's shoulders slumped heavily. He took a gulp of air from the outside without answering.

Oh crap, Tony thought. *I don't need to be in the middle of this.* He wondered if he should just step outside, or maybe tell *them* to go outside. "Hey, uh guys . . ."

"I should have left with them." Julie repeated, softer this time, drawing her knees in to her chest.

"It's getting cold in here," Tony told Carter, needing to change the subject. Carter held the lantern in two hands, as though he were about to smash it against the floor. "I think the fresh air is good, but I'm going to get that fire going. Maybe that will help." Tony unzipped his jacket and draped it over Sid's chest as an extra blanket. "Maybe some heat will help."

Carter nodded and set the lantern back on the foot-locker, before returning to wadding up the remainder of the newspaper. He didn't reply, and instead used a match to light the twisted stick of paper. He dabbed the flame around the base of the teepee. It was a good fire—the twigs lit instantly, popping like corn kernels, and the sharp scent of fresh pine was an improvement. It took only another minute before one of the logs caught, and he knew the wood was incredibly dry. It would burn hot.

Smoke and hot ash flew up the chimney, but then swirled back into the room like a noxious fog.

"What the . . . ?" Tony waved the smoke away. "I must have forgot."

Carter frowned at him. "Forgot what?"

"The flue must be shut." He started forward, leaned in as close as possible, but there was nothing in the hearth, no flue to open. More smoke plumed around him, making him sneeze.

"Oh no." Carter looked up and his mouth fell open as Tony threw a chunk of snow onto the fire, but it was already too hot. The flames sizzled and spit as they devoured it. "The chimney must be blocked up."

"Shit!" Tony screeched and waved his hands faster. "Now what?" Smoke streamed out of the hearth, rolling across the floor in waves.

From the corner Sid began to cough, hard, guttural, choking spasms that wobbled Tony's legs.

"We have to get out of here!" Carter ran forward and grabbed one end of the cot. "Now!"

MATT
Location: Byers Peak
Elevation: 12,000 feet

The wind blew past him like a scream—or was he the one screaming? Matt's mouth was open but whatever sound he tried to make lodged in his throat. There was too much wind, too much air. He couldn't breathe because of all the air rushing into his face, and he thought vaguely that was the definition of irony. He couldn't begin to guess what was over that edge. Maybe a short drop into a snowbank? Maybe it wasn't nearly as bad as what he thought it was. Because someplace deep inside, the most primitive part of his brain told him what it was.

The void.

Oblivion.

An artist, under pain of oblivion, must have confidence in himself, and listen only to his real master: nature.

Matt knew Renoir was right, but at this particular moment he believed nature was trying to kill him.

"Matt!" Leah screamed, closer now, and when he

craned his neck around he saw her sliding headfirst in an attempt to catch up to him. "Use this!" She was coming in fast, at an angle—like a torpedo aiming itself at the side of a ship. "The pole! Dig it in! Now!"

She launched it hard as a spear, as if she were attempting to skewer him straight through. She didn't miss. It hit Matt handle first in the side, and despite his shock at her actions, he had enough presence of mind to hang on to it.

"Punch it in!"

Leah rolled away, jumping like a cat onto her knees. Drawing herself up for leverage, she used both hands to bring the remaining ski pole down, piercing the glacier with a ferocious grunt. She jerked to a stop with such violence that only then did Matt understand how fast they were moving.

He wrapped the pole loop around his wrist just as he hit another rock, spinning him away like a released top. The pole clattered dumbly at his side.

"Matt! Do it now!"

He would have to let go of his phone, and with a wail and a heave he rolled onto his shoulder, imitating Leah's movements by bringing the pole down in a two-handed grip as if he was driving down a sledgehammer. One word burst from his mouth as the steel tip punctured the ice.

"Hold!"

It was a command, a prayer, a magic spell.

And it worked. Sort of.

The metal tip crunched through, but the combination

of Matt's weight and speed broke the fiberglass shaft. It splintered, almost ripping in two. His grip against the pole crushed the phone, snapping it in half like a stale cracker, showering the ice with pieces of black plastic and glass. But he still didn't stop, only slowed down enough to fall face-first onto the ice.

Here goes another tooth, he thought stupidly as the impact sent a fresh burst of blood into his mouth. Or maybe he had just bitten straight through his tongue. But he wasn't thinking about pain—he was thinking that he was still sliding.

The metal pick made a crevice—another widening crack that spread apart with crunching sounds as he bore down, and all his thoughts crystallized into one.

How close to the edge?

He needed a better grip, but didn't dare pull the pole out now.

Blue streaks in the ice underneath him, little rivers of water trickling under the surface. Then flecks of black rocks.

Those weren't rocks. They were phone shards, the one thing he had counted on for rescue. And he had just destroyed it.

A flash of yellow flew in front of his face, hitting his forehead with a heavy thud. Bright yellow with blue ribbons of nylon woven through it, and it took him a second to understand it was a rope.

"Matt! Grab it!"

With one hand he wound it quickly around his wrist, while the other remained in a death grip around the pole. The rope went taut, and Matt finally slowed to a stop. He wanted to cry. He wanted to puke. But most of all he wanted to look. *Don't do that*, he thought. *Just don't look.*

But he did. He had to.

Ten feet. That's how close he was to the edge. The wind roared below him, sounding like an angry, whining child that didn't get what it wanted, that didn't get him. "Okay Matt!" Leah yelled from somewhere above him, but he kept his head down, too petrified to respond. "I want you to wrap the rope around the pole. Make a knot!"

The rope was hard as a metal bar against his arm, though not too painful thanks to the cushion of his parka. He used the rope's extra length to wrap and tie a knot around the pole.

"Do you see that big boulder over there?" Leah called.

"Over where?" He croaked, staring at a small green and silver shard in front of his face. A piece of his SIM card—all that was left of his phone. The message his dad sent was gone, along with every photo and video and contact, which gave him a fleeting sensation of having already been erased. Like he hadn't existed in the first place, or had just been a figment of someone else's dream. But now he was awake—horribly, fantastically, unflinchingly awake. He didn't move, he didn't shout or cry or do anything other than listen to the roar of blood in his ears. The fear of gravity was paralyzing.

"To your left! Twenty feet over!"

He turned his head with infinite slowness and saw what she meant. Where he was currently located the glacier had narrowed to a ten-foot-wide alley, but twenty feet away were rock-solid boulders and granite crags. *Safety.*

He just had to reach it.

He glanced up. Leah had the rope looped around a boulder. She sat astride it, using her body to hold the rope fast, and Matt knew at the very least he could take comfort in the fact that even if he did plummet to his death, he wouldn't pull her down with him.

He started to move.

First arms. Then feet. The boulder he was heading for was directly to his left, and he didn't even bother to try to climb up. He would only slip, so instead he went sideways, inching along on his belly like a worm.

Hand, leg, chest, stomach. He flattened himself further, becoming one with the surface, oozing along like a human puddle.

One foot. Two. Three. He stopped. Breathed. Stared at the rock. There was only wind and his heartbeat. His ears throbbed, so did his throat, which was so tight and thick he couldn't even swallow his spit without pain.

Five feet. Seven. He didn't look back. He didn't look up. He didn't even blink.

Ten feet. *Halfway there,* he thought. Every muscle burned. His toes cramped up in his boots, spasmed and flexed into rigid claws. He held the pose.

"You're almost there, Matt."

Leah didn't yell, and it didn't sound like an encouragement. Instead, it reminded him of how he would talk to a frightened animal to keep it calm, which in a way was what she was doing. Strangely, it helped.

Twelve. Thirteen. Fourteen. He forced himself to slow down and pay attention, to think carefully about every movement he made. Right here. Put his hand here. He watched every inch in front of his face. The dirt-streaked ice. Wet crystals of snow on his gloves. The stiff nylon of the rope cutting into his wrist. But he kept it taut, no slack allowed as he crept forward. Just like the glacier, his motion was almost invisible.

Sixteen. Seventeen.

Closer. Closer. Closer. *Inch by inch, life's a cinch. Yard by yard, it's hard.*

He couldn't remember who said that, but he didn't think it mattered anymore.

Eighteen. Nineteen. His gloved fingertips touched rock, and even though it was slick with damp, the friction was an amazing relief from the ice.

But he didn't dare hurry. Still on his stomach, he twisted sideways until his boots were wedged up behind a boulder, and only after he curled himself into a ball around the back of it and tested its solidity did he relax.

Then he began to shake. Outside and inside. Fingers trembled, eyeballs twitched, even his teeth chattered. He had to press his hands against his mouth to make it stop.

"Good job," Leah said, her voice still calm and steady. "Now climb up here."

What? Matt thought incredulously, still pressing his gloves against his face. *She wants me to what?* "I can't."

"Yes, you can. And you have to."

His pulse felt like that of an extremely out of shape person sprinting up ten flights of stairs. "Give me a minute."

"We don't have a minute."

The sleet hit his nose and cheeks when he removed his gloves. Little ice pellets peppered the ground around him, sounding like crackling static. "What now?"

"Storm."

"You're kidding?"

"Snowstorm coming," Leah repeated in the same dispassionate tone. "Get up here now. We need to get out of this glacier field."

There was no emotion in her voice at all, as if she were making small talk about the weather. Then again, she *was* talking about the weather, and Matt had to wonder if she was crazy or had some kind of brain damage. Who slid headfirst down a glacier? Who the hell was this girl?

Then came the answer.

Someone who just saved your life. Someone you should probably listen to.

Keeping the rope tight, he started to climb.

TONY

Location: Abandoned NFS cabin,
Arapaho National Forest
Elevation: 9,000 feet

"If we put it out we might not get it going again!" Tony held up the three remaining matches from the box.

"But there's too much smoke!" Julie coughed as she wafted the thick plumes out the door with her jacket, but it didn't improve the interior of the cabin. Soon it would be a total fog of poison. They had already removed the cot—with Sid still lying on it—the footlocker, and the remainder of their supplies and gear. They even took out the chair.

"It's the chimney!" Carter rushed back in, almost colliding with Julie. "Totally blocked! God knows what! Maybe a nest, maybe a dead animal."

"Can't we burn through it?" Tony held his breath, hating the idea of smothering the flames. It had been too easy to get the fire started the first time; he knew it had been a lucky break.

"I shoved a stick up it as hard as I could." Carter had

his ski goggles down and his sweatshirt pulled up over his nose, resembling some sort of postapocalyptic fugitive. "Rock solid. Whatever it is, it's not coming out."

Still, Tony stood there holding the box of matches, wavering. "Maybe the rescuers will see it?"

"Well, they'll smell it anyway. But we need to put it out," Carter said finally, trying not to gag. "The last thing we need is for the whole damn place to burn down."

"Yeah," Julie coughed, trying to breathe through her gloves. "Let's put it out."

"Why don't you go get some snow," Carter told her, somewhat gently. He looked like he was going to put a hand on her head, as if to pet her, and Tony hoped that whatever was going on between them would be forgotten now. They had other concerns. "Fill up a bucket."

"We don't have a bucket."

"Just improvise."

Julie trudged out. Tony had the distinct impression she would have slammed the door shut if it hadn't already been kicked off its hinges during the evacuation. She was frustrated, obviously—but then, she wasn't the only one. She was mad at Carter, feeling guilty about Dylan, upset she couldn't do anything to help Sid, and apparently regretting she hadn't left with Matt and Leah. Tony knew this because he felt the exact same way. Still, he wanted to let Carter know he was on his side, that he was here to help. "Women," he said, attempting some type of camaraderie, but Carter didn't answer.

Instead he slumped his shoulders. "It was a good try," Carter said, dejected. "Don't beat yourself up about it." Then he turned and headed out, leaving Tony to wonder which side to take, if any. He knew Julie blamed Carter for the mess they were in. But the whole plan had been Dylan's—the weekend, the route, the cabin. And it had been Dylan who insisted they take that last run. If it hadn't been Carter to start the avalanche, it probably would have been someone else. It could have been Tony, though he refused to dwell on that idea. It just was a freak accident, he decided.

Only two things concerned him now—his brother and his best friend. But he knew there was nothing he could do for Matt. *Matt's on his own*, Tony thought. Sid was his brother. Sid needed him. And as he watched the dying flames flicker and fade out, he knew he would have to start making some decisions. *Pragmatic* would be the word Matt would use. He would need to be, above all things, pragmatic.

Tony hurried out of the cabin, took off his coat, and tied the arms together, making a pouch. Improvisation had always been a skill he possessed and now he put it to use, quickly scooping snow inside it until it was full. He carried it back inside and dumped the whole pile on the smoking mess, noting with some satisfaction the sound it made. Hot grease in a pan, crackling and popping. Which made Tony hungry. Soon the sizzle stopped and the coals died, smothered by ice.

When soot-stained water puddled onto the floor in front of him, Tony had decided. All that mattered now was keeping Sid alive. And if Carter and Julie got in his way he would do whatever it took. Whatever that meant. He picked up a log from the unused pile, the exact shape and size of a cudgel, one end gnarled into a thick knot. *Whatever needs to be done,* he thought. *That's what I'll do.*

MATT

Location: Byers Peak
Elevation: 11,000 feet

By the time Leah and Matt got off the north face of the mountain an hour later, it was snowing heavily. The sky around them was white and swirling, like the inside of the storm clouds themselves. Leah led them behind a wall of granite rock the size and shape of a semitruck. Finally out of the wind, Matt collapsed into a heap, grateful just to stop moving. Leah removed a small red square from her pack, unfolded it into a tarp, and by using the weight of some smaller rocks near their feet, pinned it down. With the edge secured she flipped the rest of the sheet over them, making a crude tent. Instantly, Matt felt warmer. The red nylon was thin but effective, and Matt helped drape it over their heads and shoulders. They flattened their backs against the boulder to keep it from shifting.

"We'll have to sit tight for a while," Leah said. "Until the storm passes."

Matt wasn't about to argue; he felt he might fall asleep just sitting there. "How long do you think that will be?"

"Maybe an hour. Clouds are moving pretty fast."

He wondered how she knew that. He wanted to sleep, but everything hurt, especially his head and stomach. He hadn't eaten anything since late afternoon, and he couldn't remember the last time he'd ever missed a meal. A huge goose egg had sprouted on the back of his skull and he fingered it gingerly, hoping he hadn't given himself a mild concussion. Concussed people were not supposed to go to sleep, he'd read somewhere. The lump throbbed under his thumb, keeping time with his pulse.

"We'll have to go around," Leah continued. "We're on the wrong side of the mountain now."

Matt also couldn't understand how she knew this, since the visibility in the storm was nil, but he nodded anyway. Underneath his hand, the lump seemed to have swollen to the size of a tennis ball. "Thanks." He dropped his head.

"For what?"

"For back there." He didn't want to say it—he was too embarrassed. He hadn't listened to her, and because of that he'd almost killed them both.

"Oh," Leah said distractedly. "Sure." It sounded like she went around saving people every day, the way other people hold open doors or let someone else ahead of them in the checkout line. No big deal.

"It's so weird," Matt blurted.

"What's weird?"

"I mean, what I'm trying to say . . ." He exhaled hard. "I don't know. I'm just really sorry, that's all. I shouldn't have come with."

"What do you mean?"

"You would have been better off without me along."

"No way." Leah shook her head and Matt felt the plastic slide over his. "Why would you say that?"

"But I don't know what I'm doing. I should have gotten the call through."

"You did get the call through."

Matt squeezed his fists, an instinctive inward cringe he always did when he failed at something. "I got cut off."

"That's not your fault."

"But . . ."

"*Believe* me, Matt. You'll *know* when you really mess up." Leah got serious. She spoke slowly, evenly, putting equal weight on each word. To make sure he listened to her. To make sure he really understood. "Because that will be the last thing you do. Carter was right. No one should go out here alone. This place doesn't give you second chances."

Matt thought he'd already been given a second chance—actually a third. "How did you know what to do?"

"I didn't." In the darkness he saw her outline bend forward, as if she was trying to put her head into her lap. She cradled it in her hands—elbows on her knees. The ground was cold and solid beneath them, and it made Matt's lower back ache in a distinctly painful way. Leah didn't speak for a minute and Matt wondered if she'd fallen asleep.

"Just lucky, I guess," she murmured. "Lucky like you." She sat up then, lifted the corner of the tarp, checking outside. The wind wasn't as loud now, more like a whine instead of a howl. "Carter put the rope in my pack. I told him I wouldn't need it, but he insisted."

"You guys are close, aren't you?" A small gust curled in under the tarp. The sharp cold stung his nostrils, and he saw the moonlight was back, shimmering off the sheet of snow like a spotlight.

"Carter's the only one I trust," she confessed. "He's always been on my side. He's always looked out for me."

"It must be nice," Matt said slowly, "to have a brother like that."

"Yeah." Leah pulled the tarp back farther, watching the sky. "Some days, it was the only thing . . ." She stopped and dropped the sheet, turning toward him. "I think the storm's done. Went on to the east." Her hair brushed his cheek; it smelled like mint leaves. And snow.

Matt wanted her to finish her thought, if only to understand her better. *It was the only thing what?* "I guess I wouldn't know."

"Know what?"

"Having a brother. I'm an only child."

"Oh yeah?" Leah didn't comment on this, but promptly changed the subject. "I'm hungry. You hungry?"

"Starving."

"Okay, then." Leah shrugged off her pack. "What's for dinner?"

"Didn't you bring anything?" Matt rummaged through down to the bottom of his pack, horrified. His first thought: *She doesn't have anything to eat?*

Second thought: *How much do I have left?*

Third thought: *I have to share it?*

Fourth: *I'm not sharing.*

Fifth: Complete utter burning shame (not really a thought, more like an unpleasant physical reaction).

Sixth: *I should be giving her all my food.*

"Here's what I have." Leah retrieved four cans of Rainier beer and a small packet of beef jerky—the spicy chipotle kind. One king-size Twix candy bar, a small bag of trail mix, and two clementine oranges.

"That's it?" Matt almost drooled when the golden foil of the Twix wrapper caught the light.

"Afraid so."

"Interesting diet," Matt said. "Alcohol. Meat. Sugar. I can't believe you brought beer."

"I forgot I packed it. Might as well not waste it." Leah smiled as if he'd just made a good joke.

"Guess so. I'm getting sick of eating snow anyway." Matt removed the rest of his stash, a left-over sandwich and a peanut butter granola bar, adding it to the pile.

"Now that's what I call a picnic." Leah cracked open an aluminum can and handed him another.

Matt took a long gulp, which was delicious—the most

delicious thing he'd ever tasted. He drained the entire can in twenty seconds.

"Slow down, sonny. Don't get tipsy."

"Sonny?" His throat burned, but in a good way. "You talk like you're sixty years old or something."

She laughed. "Carter says that too. I'm the oldest teenager in the world."

"So how old are you? If you're Carter's younger sister..."

"Seventeen," she replied, laughing at the surprise in his voice. "But I'll be eighteen this summer."

"But you live with Carter and Sid?" His question was innocent enough, but it implied a hundred more.

"Yeah." She sipped her beer. "For a while now I have." She tore open the pack of jerky, pulled out a thick piece, and offered him the rest.

"B-but you're not legally an adult," he stammered. "Can you even do that?"

"I guess I can," she said. "Because I did."

"But what about your parents? They just let you move out?"

Leah turned the can in her hand as if she was reading the ingredients list. Then, instead of answering, she asked him a question. "Would your parents let you move out?"

"Huh? No. Of course not. No way." Matt briefly entertained this idea, but it was so odd, so out of his normal way of thinking, it never would have occurred to him. Then again, his own father had done exactly that. Moved out. His face went hot and he felt slightly sick, as though the ground had fallen away. "Why would I?"

She didn't reply to that either, which left him to answer his own question. Why would he move out? For freedom? To be an adult on his own? To have his own place, be a man, to come and go as he pleased? He would be eighteen in two months, and he knew his mother was planning a big party. She always did stuff like that. Ever since he could remember, and the bigger the better. Balloons. Streamers. Piñatas. A cake with three layers. Invited all the relatives, invited all the neighbors. "Mattie," his mom was fond of saying, "even the little things are worth celebrating." That time he'd complained that they didn't have to invite the whole neighborhood over to celebrate the fact that he'd learned to ride a bike without training wheels. He'd been eight and a little behind the athletic curve. Then she went back to frosting the spokes on the bicycle-shaped cake she'd baked.

Matt chewed his beef jerky thoughtfully, already knowing the only reason to move out at seventeen was that your home was an awful place. That the people in it were awful. That they said and did awful things to one another.

He finished the beef jerky with a hard swallow. "It was bad, huh?"

Leah smiled. It was a thankful smile—a commiserating smile. Because she'd seen him figure out the answer, and that meant she didn't have to explain. He understood, even if he couldn't relate. And that was good enough. They finished the bag of jerky in silence, dividing the clementines, the Twix, and the granola bar, saving the trail mix and sandwich for later.

"Yeah, it was bad." She stood up and crushed her can expertly under her boot heel, then his, and slipped both discs back into her pack. "Time to go. Change into your hiking boots." She refolded the red nylon into a neat square.

"Already?" He pulled off the rigid ski boots and rolled out his ankles, then put on his pair of worn and infinitely more comfortable Merrells.

Leah zipped the tarp into a side pocket and changed into her own hiking boots. "We need to get off this peak. We have no tent and we're behind schedule."

It sounded to Matt like she was referring to some household chore that needed to be finished. "Do we need a tent?"

"Not if we can get back today." Leah was already climbing over the rocks, picking her way across the boulder field like one of those little marmots Matt had seen poking its head out from between the rocks. "Sun will be up soon."

He hurried (carefully) to catch up to her, ignoring the hot twists in his stomach. "Do you know where you're going?"

"Down," Leah said, pointing to a seemingly unending expanse of ice-stained rock. "We're going down." Boulders and boulders, many the size of a compact cars. It was dark, it was cold, there was no trail to speak of, and to Matt the scene before him made him remember another expression that had no author: *Out of the frying pan and into the fire.*

TONY

Location: Tent at abandoned NFS cabin,
Arapaho National Forest
Elevation: 9,000 feet

Carter's tent was only a two-person, and after they finished the assembly and positioned Sid inside, it became a
one-person. One person and a cot, to be exact.

"What time is it?" Tony sank down into a snowdrift.
His eyes burned, both from smoke and exhaustion. In the
past hour the wind had picked up, and beside the shelter
of the tent, the three of them had managed to construct
a crude, three-sided wall of snow, not quite an igloo but
better than nothing.

"A little past two, I think," Carter replied softly. For
now, Sid was sleeping, but his wheezy gasps set Tony's
teeth on edge. They could hear it through the thin nylon,
a rattling noise, thick and guttural, and Tony both wished
he'd stop making that sound and became terrified he actually might. All three of them had been awake for hours,
sitting mutely in the dark, then getting up and walking

a trail around the cabin, trying to stay warm, trying to think of what else they could do. Tony had guessed it was slightly above freezing, and since there wasn't enough room in the tent for everyone, they took turns going inside to warm up.

Once again, Tony was thankful Carter had brought a tent, though Julie said Dylan had brought one too, in case they couldn't find the cabin, and that left Tony to wonder what *would* have happened if they hadn't found it before dark. In any case, it was too polluted with carbon monoxide to be of any use to them now.

"I'm hungry," Tony said to his feet. "Can we eat yet?"

"Julie? What do we have left?"

"Hot dogs. Buns. Graham crackers. Marshmallows. Chocolate bars." She unzipped the soft-sided cooler. "And beer."

"I need one of each," Tony said. "Actually, make that two."

They parceled out the food three ways, and Tony took his share into the tent. "Sid? You sleeping?"

No answer. Tony almost dropped the hot dogs when he realized how quiet it was inside the tent. No rattle. "Sid!"

"W-what?" Sid gurgled, awakening, then shook the cot with his hacking cough, and this time Tony did drop the hot dogs. They landed with a plop on top of the sleeping bag. "Carter!" he yelled.

"You all right?" Carter poked his head in, then lifted

up the lantern. After several hours, the fuel canister was almost depleted, but the faint light revealed Sid, his eyes squeezed shut.

"What's happening?"

Carter crawled all the way in and moved the light over Sid, then pulled down the collar of Sid's shirt. Veins bulged on his neck, and his lips looked bluish in the lantern glow. "Lack of oxygen. It's getting really hard for him to breathe."

"What do we do?" Tony croaked.

"In a few hours it'll be dawn," Carter replied. "We need to take turns staying awake and monitoring him. I'm going to go out and try again for a signal." He backed himself out of the tent. "I'll come back and sit with him." He gave Tony a look. "You need to sleep too."

"I can't." Tony squeezed his brother's hand as Carter left to go try his phone, and after a few seconds Sid's coughing fit subsided. Tony tried to get him to drink something, raising his water bottle to Sid's lips, but Sid turned his head away. "Drink something," Tony said. "That'll help." He didn't know if that was true, but it seemed like it would work on a cough. Or maybe that would only make things worse. A sort of helpless rage began to rise inside him. *So this is what it's like,* he thought. *This is what it's like to watch someone you love suffer and know there's not a thing you can do about it.*

"No," Sid murmured. "It hurts. I can't."

"You have to try. Help will be here soon." He didn't

know if that was true either, but he would sit there and keep telling lies if he thought it would help. He would say anything. "It'll be morning soon." He began to talk, if only to take Sid's mind off his pain. "Matt and Leah have gotten the call through. We just have to wait for first light, that's all. Carter said they'll send rescue. Carter knows. And then, they'll find us and we'll be out of here. Safe and sound. You just have to wait a little longer, okay?"

Sid didn't answer.

"Just a little longer and we'll be safe and sound," Tony repeated, squeezing his brother's hand as though he could create a pulse by sheer will. He would be his brother's heart. He would pump the blood through his veins. Anything he needed to do. Anything at all.

"Safe and sound."

"Fine."

"Fine!"

Tony awoke with a start. Sleep gummed his eyes, and he coughed, squeezing his brother's hand in his. How long had he been asleep? Minutes? An hour? He had no idea. He leaned over Sid and held his breath, listening. Sid sounded wheezy, his breath coming in hard bursts, but it was steady. In the dark, Tony felt his brother's wrist. Pulse faster than his, but not racing.

"Just don't."

"Don't what?"

"You know what."

So that was it, Tony thought. Carter and Julie's voices were loud, sounding so incredibly close to him he flinched. He wondered if he should do something, say something. Probably. But what?

Outside, Julie laughed, high and shaky. "I have no idea what you mean, Carter." She said his name like she was chewing on gravel, crunching down on the consonants. Listening to her, Tony thought she was delirious, feverish, or even drunk. Again, he wondered how long he'd been asleep.

"Julie, why don't you just rest." Carter sighed, sounding like he was trying to placate a toddler.

"And why don't you just leave me alone, Carter. For once, please. Just. Leave. Me. Alone."

Whoa. Tony sat up. He dropped Sid's hand and unzipped the flap, a poorly worded plea forming on his lips. "Uh, hey guys . . ."

Carter and Julie stood in the moonlight. The wind had died down and the way they faced each other reminded Tony of a duel. They didn't hear him.

"I'm not going to keep going over this." Carter crossed his arms. "I'm not gonna waste my breath. You haven't slept. You're tired and you're not thinking straight."

"Typical Carter. Always ready to take charge, forever the perfect Boy Scout." Tony heard Julie's voice crack like the snapping of twigs. She let out a long breath—as if it had been trapped in her lungs for years. "Stop telling me why I feel the way I feel."

Carter shook his head, and Tony could have sworn he saw a light smile break his stern lips. "You were always a little rough in the morning—when you were still sleepy." Carter chuckled softly—tenderly. Tony's ears turned red at the sound. He tried covering his face with the tent flap. This was more than one friend arguing with another. *A LOT more.* Carter reached toward Julie's check.

"Don't!" she snapped.

Tony saw Carter's shoulder's drop, then his head turn away in shame. Tony didn't really know either of them, or what had happened—was happening—between the two of them now. But what he did know was that Carter's hesitant touch set Julie off. She lifted her chin and looked at Carter as if he had just kicked her puppy.

"What are you thinking?" Julie shot back. "Dylan's gone, and you . . ."

"Stop it. Stop it. Stop it. Stop it," Tony said, but it only came out in a whisper. "Please," he added a bit louder.

Julie buried her head in her hands. Carter stepped closer, then thought better of it. His boots *crunch-crunched* in the snow.

"You took his beacon," Julie whispered in muffled words, her eyes glazed over from either tears or exhaustion, Tony couldn't tell. *Maybe both.*

"Don't you dare . . . ," Carter began. He knew what was coming, and so did Tony.

"*You* took Dylan's beacon! You . . . did it on purpose?"

"I didn't," Carter yelled back, but it sounded strangled,

like he was choking on the words. "I didn't take his beacon! He gave it to me! He knew what he was doing!"

Tony swallowed hard. If Carter hadn't asked them about their beacons, he wouldn't have known Matt didn't have one. Tony hadn't even thought to mention it. But Carter yelled at Dylan and Dylan handed it over. If that hadn't happened, Matt would have been the one who died. They never would have found him in time. Tony was suddenly dizzy at how one innocent comment had become the difference between life and death.

"And now look!" Julie screamed, waving her arms as if she was trying to chop the air in half. "Now Dylan's dead!"

Carter crossed his arms, his lips pinched shut. Tony thought he heard him growl like an angry wolf, until, "Don't you put your guilt on me! H-he was m-my f-friend too," Carter stuttered. He pulled off his hat and held it in front of his face. Julie looked to the sky. Whatever guilt was nibbling at Carter, Tony knew it was devouring Julie in one nasty gulp. He decided he'd had enough as he crawled out of the tent.

"Carter?" Tony said. "Uh, sorry. I, um, think I fell asleep." He walked into the space between them, his back to Julie. "Carter, maybe you should sit with Sid for a while. I'll stay out here." *Give you two a break,* he added in his head.

Carter didn't reply, but immediately turned and headed to the tent, his face still hidden by his hat.

Behind him, Tony felt Julie's glare. It penetrated the

back of his head, infecting him. "You shouldn't have said that." Tony turned his face up to the dark sky. The moon was now veiled with thin clouds, as if covered with tissue paper. "You shouldn't have said that," he repeated, louder. "It wasn't Carter's fault."

Tony turned around to face her and he felt his stomach sink like a rock dropped in a pool of water. Her eyes were bloodshot, her lips chapped, and her skin burned from the wind. She wasn't exhausted, Tony realized. She was defeated—as if the mountains had beaten her, buried her under a wall of snow and she had no desire to dig herself out.

Julie's eyes opened wider. Then her mouth did, but a second later she shut it, clicking her teeth together. "You don't know anything," she finally said, but she didn't sound so sure to Tony. With another choked sob, she turned and stumbled back through the drifts, heading toward the pines.

"I know enough," Tony whispered, watching her go.

THE HUNTER
Location: 400 yards from the cabin

The wind was heavy with burning, and the cat sneezed. It snorted its nose against the snow to remove the itch, and wiped one heavy paw across its muzzle.

It did not like the smoke, and normally would have moved off, but it was the others that kept it close. Animals. Prey. A pack of four. One injured. Even from this distance and through the thick acidic air, the cat smelled it. Blood. Underneath everything it penetrated, and the cat salivated, tail twitching in anticipation. It watched the cabin from the thick cover of pines, high up on the slope. But it did not approach.

Moonlight sparkled the fresh snow, silver glitter on white. Deep, inky shadows ran long between the trees.

The voices were low, but growing louder. The cat watched as the herd bunched tight together.

It would not attempt an attack on so large a group, so it sat and watched, waiting for the right moment.

The cat rolled its long tongue, sweeping it out into a yawn, and curled up under the snow-laden boughs, tucking its long tail around it like a belt. It would wait and watch. The night would be long, but it was a patient animal.

DAY 3

MATT
Location: Byers Peak
Elevation: 9,500 feet

Dawn took a long time to arrive, but the deep navy black sky eventually dissolved away, and a neon crack of green shone at the horizon line just before the glaring ball of sun rose behind it. Small clouds strafed the sky in powder-blue and cotton candy–pink shades, and by the time they finally escaped the boulder field, the sun was fully up. Matt couldn't remember the last time he'd been so happy to see trees.

"I need to rest." He sat down by a scraggly-looking pine dusted in a fresh coating of snow. There was a sharp *cheet* above his head, and he stared up into the branches until a flash of red revealed a cardinal perched on a pinecone in the morning light, ruffling its feathers. He relaxed, but it made him anxious about what other animals were out here. It hadn't concerned him before, but that was when he was in a large group of people.

"Are there wolves in Colorado?"

"Wolves?" Leah shook her head. "No. Not here. I

don't think there have been wolves in these parts for years. Coyotes maybe." She gestured to a twisty but wide-looking streak of snowpack through the trees. It appeared to be a trail. "But there are bears. And mountain lions too."

"Mountain lions?" Matt's voice shifted up an octave.

"They're rare."

"Oh."

"It's the bears you don't want to run into. That would be very bad luck."

"Good to know." Maybe he'd been thinking about it wrong. Maybe he wasn't lucky at all. People would say he was lucky because he was still alive. But another way to look at it was that he was incredibly unlucky to be in this situation at all. It could have just been a normal ski trip. It *should* have been normal. Awesome and unforgettable, Matt thought, trudging on. His right foot throbbed—an increasing ache in his toes. He hadn't waterproofed his hiking boots, and after an hour of trekking through snow, his feet were soaked. A soft hum made him blink. It grew louder. *Music?* Behind him, Leah was singing.

"For the bears," she explained with a grin. With a pink hat on, her red hair was almost obscene in the soft morning light. "To let them know we're coming. You should sing too."

"I can't sing." He blushed, trying to remember where he'd heard the song. The melody was familiar. "What song is that, anyway?"

"Don't you know?" She swiveled her hips like a hula

dancer. "'Bump, bah dah dah! If you like piña coladas! Getting caught in the rain!'"

His face reheated, watching her curls swing down around her shoulders as she shimmied a circle in the snow. "Don't know that one." That was half true. He had heard that song before. It was a song his dad would sing in the car, and now that he knew the words, he hated it. But he couldn't think of another song he could sing, not even if his life depended on it. He started to laugh.

"What? I'm that bad?" Leah scooped up a fistful of snow, and at first Matt thought she was going to pelt him with it. But she ate it.

"No," he said. "You sing good. I mean, you sing very well." Another blush. "It's just that's the kind of music my parents listen to."

Leah shrugged. "Good music is good music."

"I guess," Matt replied, then stopped. *Two roads diverged.* Well not roads, but trails. And there was no yellow wood, only white and black with streaks of green. "Which way?" he asked. "The one less traveled?"

Leah pointed left. "How about that one?" Neither path had been traveled, at least, not by people. There were other tracks he thought he recognized—rabbits with their lopsided hop, deer with petite puncture marks, squirrels with baby-like handprints. "But I don't know if it will make all the difference," she added.

"Robert Frost was probably drunk in the woods when he wrote that," Matt said. "He liked his booze."

"Really? I didn't know that."

"Great poet, but I heard he wasn't the nicest guy."

"Sounds like my foster mom," Leah said quickly. "Except she was only good at being a drunk. Not at any kind of poetry. At least, not that I'd ever seen."

Matt flinched. "Oh yeah?" He was afraid to say anything—almost afraid to even breathe. Usually when people offer up a confession like that, they are just getting started.

"But man, she could put it away." Leah tromped along, watching the clouds, which had thickened up again in the space of an hour. "Beer, wine, gin, whiskey, vodka. She was an equal opportunity drunk, but I think gin was her favorite." Matt watched her watch the building weather. He wondered if that meant there would be another storm. "Which is weird, because she'd get all weepy and emotional. Normally, she was a total hard ass." She stopped, eyes flickering at him expectantly, waiting for his reaction.

"How long were you in foster care?"

"On and off since I was little," Leah said. "I'll age out soon, like Carter did when he turned eighteen."

"Age out?"

"When I become a legal adult. No more foster crap to deal with."

"Oh." He hoped his face wasn't as red as it felt. Even his eyeballs felt swollen and tight. "That's good, right?"

Her reply was too soft to hear, and when he opened

his mouth, trying to think of the right thing to say, a distant rumble penetrated the quiet. And it wasn't thunder. "Is that what I think it is?"

"Yes!" Leah leaped forward, ducking her head around for an open spot between the trees. "And I think it's coming this way!"

Frantic, Matt ran forward, seeing nothing but snow and bark and pine needles. White. Green. White. "We need to get out in the open! We have to make them see us!" He jogged sideways, looking for the most white space between the trees, and when he saw the huge fir tree surrounded by snow out in the open, it beckoned to him like a lighthouse. "There!" He knew if he could get to that tree and climb it, the people in the helicopter would see him. His parka and snow pants were navy blue and black, respectively, which was an unfortunate choice. At a moment like this he wished he was dressed head to toe in blaze orange. "C'mon Leah!" Adrenaline was everywhere, fizzing his blood to a boil, and despite his hunger, fatigue, and aching feet, he hurled himself forward, sprinting over drifts.

You can do this, he thought. He was doing it, even though he no longer felt his legs move. His feet were hard stumps in his boots, but he kept running. Ten yards, thirty, fifty. Leah yelled behind him, but he couldn't wait for her—the sound was louder—*batabatabatabatabata.* And suddenly it was there, streaking over the treetops, flashing red and white and silver between the clouds. *Rescue.* The call had gone through. They were coming.

They needed something bright. Leah's jacket was green, but her hot pink hat would definitely catch a pilot's eye. "Leah!" Matt yelled. "Wave your hat!" He flapped his own arms, windmilling them as he burst onto the small clearing. The drifts here were ridiculous, but as he ran down the hill, he thought it looked like someplace skiers would go—a lot of deep powder and very few trees.

The helicopter was still some distance away—flying parallel to the range—but Matt could see it wasn't coming closer. It was moving off in the opposite direction. *Maybe it will make another pass,* he thought. Then he would have just enough time to climb to the treetop and shake the branches. They would have to notice that.

"Matt!"

"Hurry!" he hollered. "It'll come back around!"

"Wait! Don't!"

Ten yards. He was close; his feet sank into fresh powder that ended over his shins, the next step it went to his knees. But he didn't stop. And with two more steps, his gloves brushed the snow-draped branches.

"No!" Leah screamed.

Instantly, the ground dropped out from under him. There was *no* ground, just a widening hole. And as he fell, momentum propelled him forward, flinging him deeper into the branches. "What the hell?" he gasped.

The fresh powder around the branches had made a roof of snow around the lower half of the tree and right now Matt was crashing through it. Instinctively, his grip tightened, but the limb he grasped was flexible, bending, following him down as he fell. His brain commanded: *Don't let go. Don't let go.* He crashed against the main trunk, scrabbling with his left hand to hold on to anything that would keep him upright. Going headfirst would land him upside down in a pit of snow. *No, no, no, no, no! This can't be happening to me again!*

"Matt!" Leah screamed. "Grab the tree!"

But he was still falling, kicking with his feet, as everything collapsed with him. Under the force of his weight, the branch he stood on broke, and he slammed down to the next one. *Stay up. Stay up. Head up!*

Something sharp stabbed through his coat, under his armpit. "Ow!" Snow rained down on his head. Tree branches snapped and catapulted fluffy powder into the sky, as though they had just exploded into dust. Still, there was nothing solid underneath him, and he continued to fall. The astringent, tarry scent of tree sap was everywhere. Boughs splintered and cracked. Limbs shuddered as he grabbed and kicked, his vision swimming around him so fast it was as if he was inside a storm. A cyclone of snow and pine needles.

Wham! He finally hit something hard enough to stop his freefall. The ground. Snow pelted his back, and he pedaled his legs, pumped his arms, and pushed himself frantically to his knees, determined to get himself upright before he was buried. Sticky branches and fir needles stung his cheeks and poked his eyes as he thrashed about in the soft snow. When he reached the trunk, a huge wall of snow caved in behind him.

He pressed his face so tight to the bark he could taste it.

"Matt!" Leah was above him; she sounded close.

"I'm here!" Fear distilled his thoughts into one. She could fall in too. "Don't come over here!" he screeched.

"I know! It's a tree well!"

What the hell is that? By tilting his chin up, he saw gray sky through the thick branches, and around him walls of snow, which were still sliding toward him. It *was* like being at the bottom of a well. A well that was collapsing on him.

"Are you hurt?"

"No, I don't think so!"

"Can you get out?"

"It's deep!" The snow around the base of the tree was piled to his waist, and he shifted back and forth to make space. "I'm about fifteen feet down!" His hands, thankfully, were free, and that gave him the ability to scoop away snow until he could bring his knees up. He pulled carefully on a broad limb, hoisting himself up slowly, and as he did he felt the snow slide down to fill the hole he left. He clung to the trunk like a frightened squirrel.

"That's deep!"

"No shit!" *I'm in deep shit. And by shit I mean snow.*

"Are you by the tree?"

"I'm ON it!" He was suddenly painfully aware that it was the only thing that saved him.

"Really? Can you climb it?"

"I'm going to try!" Fatigue was a heavy blanket, paining him even to speak. How would he have the strength to get out?

"Do it!" Leah shouted. "I can't get any closer! If you climb up halfway I can throw you the rope!"

"Okay!" Matt's fingers were swollen, burning bright with cold, and he climbed gingerly, scraping against the bark. The higher he went the less space he had to maneuver, and by the time he got above the well, he was debating how he would manage the feat. It wasn't like climbing up some sturdy-limbed oak or maple tree. Everything bent under his weight, throwing him off balance. Branches slapped and poked him. Sap stung his windburned cheeks. Cursing, he kept going.

"I see you!" Leah shouted as his head emerged between the branches. "Can you catch the rope?"

"Uh." She was ten feet away, holding the loop of rope like a lasso. "I'll try."

"Do or do not," she deadpanned. "There is no try."

"Thanks, Yoda."

"No problem." She swung the coil, ready to hurl the knotted end at him. "Okay, get ready!"

Six throws later it got close. But he wouldn't let go to reach for it. On the seventh try it snagged a branch next to his shoulder and he grabbed it, winding it tight around his wrist. "Got it!" He tugged it to his chest. "Now what?"

"Now you have to jump."

"How?" His feet were balanced on several limbs, each one swaying under his weight. The farther he moved from the trunk, the more unstable his perch became. But he would have to jump. There was no other way out.

"Turn around," Leah ordered. "Push off and jump out. I'll pull you when you're in the air."

It sounded crazy. But Matt couldn't think of a better plan. He seriously doubted there was one.

"Don't worry!" she told him. "The snow is deep."

"I know!" A wave of nausea broke across his face as he remembered the tumbling sensation, the stomach-dropping fright of almost going headfirst into the hole. "That's the whole problem!" He clenched his teeth at the image of snow piling down around him. A stabbing pain started behind his ears, throbbing in time with his pulse, and he stayed crouched in the tree like a gargoyle, immobile with thoughts of disaster.

"You just have to jump out! That should get you clear!"

That should get him clear. Or was it: That *should* get him clear.

Leah snapped the rope. "Jump out like you're jumping out of a plane!"

"I've never jumped out of a plane! And I don't plan to!"

"That helicopter's not coming back!" Leah hollered. "At least, not anytime soon. So you might as well jump." A second later she laughed. "That's a quote for you! Van Halen!"

"I know that." He didn't see how she could find any humor in the situation.

"Of course you do, Matt. You know everything! You even know about tree wells."

Smart-ass, he thought, wondering if she was trying to piss him off on purpose. Make him forget his fear. Make him just do it already. "Yeah, I have personal experience. I'm practically an expert."

"Great! Let's go, then." She pulled the rope, looping a section around her glove, and Matt saw it was tied around her waist, finished with a complicated-looking knot centered below her chest. "Jump out, keep your arms close to your chest but in front of you."

"Okay." He didn't ask why.

"Count of three, okay?" She stepped back into a fighting stance, removing the slack between them. "One . . . two . . ."

"Three!" He jumped, pushing off as hard as he dared, busting through pine boughs that threatened to slap him back. He looked straight ahead, focusing first on the mountain horizon line, then on Leah's face, some distance away but zooming closer. His arms jerked forward as if he were being pulled up on water skis as she heaved him back, like she was trying to win the ultimate tug-of-war contest. She yanked the rope so hard she landed flat on her back.

He cleared the tree and ended up in a modest-size drift, sinking down onto his hands and knees. After the initial panic subsided, he crawled forward, panting like a dog. Then he turned his head and started retching. Fortunately, nothing came out.

Leah sat back up, leaving a strange snow angel impression behind her. "You know, I didn't want to say this before, but ninety percent of people who get trapped in a tree well can't get out."

Matt wiped his mouth on his sleeve. "Can't get out?"

"Not by themselves."

"Ninety percent?" He focused on the horizon line, waiting for the nausea to drift off.

"Looks like you're the lucky ten." She wound the rope into a tight loop. "I think you're the luckiest person I've ever met."

"We only met two days ago."

"That's long enough to know."

"Well, I'm lucky you're with me."

She shrugged. "I think you would've gotten out on your own."

"Maybe. Maybe not." He cringed thinking about it, then the image of his near plummet off the cliff returned. "I'm very, very glad Carter made you bring the rope."

"Me too." Leah nodded. "I have a new appreciation for its uses. I'll never take a long piece of nylon cord for granted again." Gratitude lit her face like a shaft of sunlight, and even Matt saw what she was thinking. Because he was thinking it too.

Thank you, Carter.

JULIE
Location: Heading east from abandoned NFS cabin, Arapaho National Forest
Elevation: 9,000 feet

Julie had not intended to leave. But then, she was not the type of person who intended a lot of things. Spontaneous by nature, these things just seemed to *happen* to her, often without her consciously deciding anything. It was near dawn when she'd found herself skiing away from the boys in one quiet moment, and only when a crack of tree limbs in the distance caught her attention did she even notice how far she'd gone. She stopped suddenly, like a sleep-walker who'd just been awakened.

She turned her ski tips, rested on her poles, then checked the phone she'd taken from Carter's pack while he slept. No signal. Not yet. But the compass worked, and Julie was enormously pleased to see that she was going in the right direction. *This way,* she thought. She didn't feel that bad about taking it; Tony still had his, and if she could climb up above the tree line she was certain the phone would work. Where Matt and Leah might have failed, Julie was determined to succeed.

I'll get up to where it'll work, she told herself, not dwelling on the fact that Matt and Leah had left hours ago for that specific task. But something must have happened to them, and in Julie's mind it was because she hadn't gone with them. She gritted her teeth; her stomach growled so loudly in the quiet that it startled her. But it wasn't unpleasant. For Julie, hunger was a good thing. It made her feel sharper somehow, putting everything into focus. Letting her forget about Carter and what happened in Dylan's apartment two nights before. What she *let* happen. But Carter was, well, Carter. Her first . . . everything. She let herself have one moment of weakness. One moment of nostalgia. And now she could never take it back. Carter was right. She felt guilty. She shouldn't have said what she did. She *knew* that, but knowing it didn't really help things, not now. And drowning in her guilt wasn't going to fix anything either. She had to act—leave her regret and shame behind.

Another crack in the distance, sharper this time, and she swiveled around trying to find its location. The noise reminded Julie of a rifle report and she caught her breath in excitement. *Someone else could be out here! Hunters?* She turned her ski tips in a new direction, energy renewed. Maybe Matt and Leah *did* get a call through—there could be rescuers out there right now combing the woods. A burring whine punctured the silence around her and Julie smiled, certain that this was the sound of a snowmobile, and she pushed off vigorously into the growing light.

TONY

Location: Tent at abandoned NFS cabin,
Arapaho National Forest
Elevation: 9,000 feet

"Carter?"

"Mmrf."

"Carter, wake up!" At first Tony thought Carter was dead—a human Popsicle propped up in his thermal sleeping bag against the snow wall. Tony hesitated to touch him. His face was so pale it looked like milk, but then Tony remembered Carter's face was that pale anyway. "Carter!" He poked the side of his head reluctantly. "Wake up! I heard something!"

"W-what?" Carter opened his eyes, which were streaked bloodshot, making his irises glimmer like bright emerald chips. "Heard what?"

"Something different." Tony had been sleeping himself, bent over Sid's feet, which seemed to be the only place on his brother that wasn't injured. He hadn't meant to fall asleep again; he didn't even remember doing it.

Before, sitting out in the snow with Julie, he'd been too angry to fall asleep, and eventually she had, snoring softly in the dark. And when Carter came to relieve him, he'd only been too happy to leave the snow fort and go back to Sid. That had been at least two hours ago. Now a soft light was dissolving the dark, turning the iron gray landscape to pewter. It must be past dawn. "Something mechanical." He knew it hadn't been the wind or the trees, or an owl or woodpecker, or any other animal. "I think it might have been a helicopter."

Now Carter was fully awake. He jumped up, his sleeping bag still snugly around him so that he resembled a giant red caterpillar. "Really?"

"I think so."

Carter shimmied out and reached for his phone, which wasn't in his backpack. "Shit! Where is it?"

"It's almost six," Tony informed him, understanding what he wanted.

"Six?" Carter sounded utterly astonished by this. "Okay, okay, okay," he muttered, swiveling around while he stared at the sky. "Where did the sound come from?"

"Um." Tony followed his peering stare. "I don't know. I just know I heard something."

Batabatabatabata. The thick fluttering noise returned, and Carter spun in a circle and almost fell over. "I hear it! That's definitely a chopper!"

"I told you!" Tony was triumphant, and as he ran back to the tent to tell Sid the good news, the helicopter appeared, thundering over the treetops, red and white and shining in the sky. Tony waved his arms at it like a maniac. "Hey! Hey! Here! We're here!"

Carter swung his sleeping bag over his head in an insane dance. They would have to see that, Tony decided, but when he looked up again the helicopter was gone. "What!" he hollered. "Carter?"

"Don't worry! They saw us! They saw us!" Carter hopped up and down. "They can't land right here! Too many trees!"

"What do we do?" Tony's excitement turned to hope. *They did it. Matt did it.*

"Get Sid ready! They're coming!"

"Yes!" Tony spun around, noticing something he hadn't before. Two thin parallel lines, leading off into the trees. Fresh ski tracks. *Why would? Who . . .* Tony turned one more complete circle and stopped. *No. Nonononono-nonono!*

"Julie!" he hollered into the trees, hoping he was mistaken. But as he screamed her name, hearing only his own echo, he knew Julie had left, either too impatient to wait any longer for help or too angry at Carter to stay. Maybe a little of both, but the end result was the same. "Julie!" But the trees stayed silent.

Julie was gone.

"Sid!" Tony burst through the flap of the tent, half expecting her to be there. He blinked in the dimness, looking for her to be crouched in a corner. Nothing. No

Julie. "They're coming, Sid! The helicopter! It found us!"

But Sid didn't answer. He didn't even flinch at the shout, and when Tony stood over him, then bent down to listen, the only breath he heard was his own. He bent closer, and with shaking fingers touched his brother's neck, feeling for a pulse.

"Carter!"

MATT

Location: Unknown river
Elevation: 9,000 feet

Matt heard the river before he saw it, the steady white noise of rushing water. There was not much snow here, as if they had entered spring through a door in the forest, leaving winter behind on the mountain.

"Is that water up ahead?" Water might mean a hiking trail, a road, or best yet, other people.

"It better be." Leah began to trot in anticipation. "Maybe a river."

"Do you know which one?" He followed her through the brush. The ground was still steadily sloping down, and here it was damp and spongy, smelling like green wet cedar, loam, and dirt. Rocks jutted up between the trees like giant toadstools.

"There's probably a few streams out here," Leah said. "But I don't know what they're called."

They'd been walking all morning, and Matt had spent almost every step trying not to think about why. Instead, he concentrated his few thoughts on the simple things in front of his face. Trees. Rocks. Snow. Leah's green jacket and red curls. Things under his feet. Snow. Ice. Dirt. More snow. He kept a running tally of every twinge in his muscles, every spasm, every quivering ache. How the wind felt on his face, the sharpness of it, making tears bead up in the corners of his eyes. He concentrated on everything but the tight line of fire in his stomach. Right foot. Left foot. Don't trip on that rock. Keep your eyes open. What's that sound? A bird? A squirrel? Something else? Is that a blister growing on my pinky toe?

That was the pain he couldn't ignore. With every step his feet shuddered and burned. But he couldn't stop walking—that was not an option. He was uncomfortable, to say the least, and that made him remember what Tony had told him once, when they were running wind sprints in basketball tryouts and Matt was just about ready to stop: "Hey dude, you need to get comfortable with pain."

I just need to get comfortable with pain, Matt thought, but with every scorching step the vision came back. The edge of the cliff in the glacier field. The way it looked, how it seemed to just be waiting for him, and he tried to understand what he saw, what he'd been thinking during those last seconds when it was obvious what was going to happen. He couldn't seem to hold on to any specific thought. It was like trying to hold water in your hands. Eventually it all trickled out, leaving you with wet palms and nothing to drink. In some ways it felt as if he'd dreamed it, or that it happened to someone else. A scene from an old movie. Not real. It wasn't real. He was not real. How did he know he was here anymore? Did you even know it when you died?

Matt's tailbone radiated pain through his butt. He was on the ground, sitting with his legs twisted underneath him like a pretzel, but he didn't remember falling.

"Matt?" Leah's face was close in front of his. "What are you doing?"

"Umm." Pink and green blobs flashed in front of his face. "I think ... I'm not sure ... I don't ... know ..."

"Did you faint?"

"Uh ..." He huffed and pulled himself together into a crouch and watched the blobs disappear. "Maybe," he said slowly. "Maybe it was the beer."

"Huh," Leah said. "You don't look like a lightweight."

Was that a fat joke? Then he remembered he wasn't fat anymore, not even considered overweight. Technically he was in great physical condition, according to his gym teacher and basketball coach. The only problem was right now he couldn't feel it. Right now, he figured, he couldn't even spell his own name. "P-probably elevation. Not used to this kind of exercise."

"Me either," Leah agreed, but Matt saw she wasn't breathing hard. Not like he was. And she barely broke a sweat. After their beer break he had lifted her pack, which turned out to be just as heavy as his. Another reason he decided to carry the rest of the food. To even out the weight, he told himself. To be fair, not greedy. "But we're getting close."

"You think?"

"Water's always a good sign." Leah helped him up. "We can follow it. Probably find a road, or maybe it will lead us down to a lake."

"Water's good?"

"Yeah. Water usually means people."

And people meant rescue.

Matt had never been much of a people person, but right now he couldn't imagine a more welcome sight.

"How many more miles?" The pines weren't thick here, and the trees hadn't leafed out. But some bushes were newly green at the tips, buds swollen and ready to pop with the next warm day.

"Don't know," Leah replied. "We didn't go the right way down the peak."

That was the understatement of the year.

The sound of water grew louder, but Matt didn't see anything until he followed Leah around a crag of rock. There, twenty feet below, he saw it, wild and fast. It looked like something people would pay money to raft down— all white water, boiling and foaming over the rocks. It was stunningly beautiful, starting a different kind of ache in Matt's stomach. An ache that wasn't hunger but wasn't something he could name, and he stood staring at the force of the water. There was no way across it.

Leah scanned downstream. "We'll follow it a bit to see if there's a way to cross over."

"We have to cross it?" It was impossible not to look at that water and imagine the temperature, possibly a few degrees above freezing. Matt shivered.

"We're still too high, and the roads and trails will be on the opposite side, heading down into the valley." She adjusted her pack and squared her shoulders. "We just need to find the right spot."

"It looks like it's thirty feet wide."

"I know." Leah slid around another boulder and picked her way down to the river's edge, looking for a path along the water. "But there might be an easy spot some ways down. Maybe even a bridge if we're lucky."

He scudded his way along the slick rocks, knowing with one slip he'd end up in ice-cold rapids. Swimming was not the issue; nothing about the water looked like a good idea, except maybe for drinking. He was still thirsty, despite all the snow, and when he scrambled his way down to a wide spot on the bank he leaned over and dipped his hand into a swirling eddy. He was right about the temperature, so cold it burned. Imagining the taste, saliva pooled in his mouth. He cupped his palm up to his lips.

"Don't!" Leah barked. "Don't drink that!"

"Why?" The water ran out through his fingers. "What's wrong?" He'd been eating snow all day without getting sick.

Leah uncapped her water bottle, which Matt saw was

not at all like the plastic one he carried. Hers was blue, with a thick tube inside. "This has a filter." She filled the bottle. "You really don't want a case of Giardia."

"What's that?" It sounded like something Italian, like something his mom would make for dinner. Giardia with a side of garlic bread. He stared hesitantly at the water bottle.

"Pretty nasty little parasite. You really don't want it."

Matt took a long drag through the straw. Then another. Once he started it was hard to stop.

"Drink as much as you need," she said. "You look like you..."

A rustle in the bushes behind him cut her off. Two shiny eyes, like small black marbles, blinked out from the green. Black wet nose. Perfect half-moon ears. Fur the color of dusted cinnamon.

Matt almost dropped his bottle. "A little baby bear. Leah, look."

"Hey little guy." Leah squatted down and offered out her hand, as if to greet a small dog. "Hey there."

The bear blinked, then sneezed and opened its mouth, smiling with tiny teeth and shiny pink gums. "Where is his...," Leah began, suddenly realizing her mistake. She popped back up, eyes darting up and down the ravine as she backed away. "Mother...," she whispered. "Oh no."

Matt backed up so quickly he almost sat down, nearly ending up in the water. It didn't look very deep at the edge, but it was running so fast he was sure it would knock him

over if he fell in. His eyes stayed locked on the trees surrounding the ravine. *Where is she? She has to be close.*

He was right. High up on the ridge, branches bent in a
deep wave, then snapped. The mother bear burst through
the underbrush, and even from this distance Matt could
see how her tiny glowing eyes fixed on him. With a
hair-raising snarl she hurtled down the slope like a demon
just released from the gates of hell.

JULIE

Location: Ascending Bills Peak
Elevation: 9,500 feet

Julie had been following a narrow trail up between the aspen and cedar, climbing steadily with her head down, and watched as the snow beneath her skis changed from navy to violet to pink to gray to a final powder puff white. Sunrise. She stopped, panting heavily, and removed her ski mask. She was almost above the tree line. Each breath was harder than the last, and when she spied a large patch of white between the trees, for a moment she hallucinated a lake. It shimmered under the rising sun with a prismatic rainbow of light.

Strangely entranced, she pushed herself until she stood at its edge. Not a lake, but a river of snow. The avalanche. The field, in the early dawn light, looked calm. Not the horrible devastation she recalled from a day ago. *Not even a day,* she reminded herself, biting down on her lip. *Dylan, where are you?* She knew she shouldn't go out there. It was unsteady ground and it could break again. She knew that. But she was also angry. Not really at Carter, even though he'd taken the brunt of it. *Why did you have to be so careless, Dylan? You knew better than that. Why?* The anger was a bitter stew in her stomach, hot and roiling. What good was it to be angry at Dylan—he'd already paid for his mistake, and she bit down harder on her lip until she tasted the rust of her blood. *It's not right to be angry,* she reasoned with herself. But the logic would not follow. She still was angry—angry with herself most of all.

Her eyes scanned up the slope, looking for anything other than snow and ice. A flicker of red. Something there. Dylan had a red hat, didn't he? She shook her head and blinked, not able to remember. Had it been red or blue? She pushed herself out onto the slope, cautiously at first, then skied quickly over to the small splotch of color. Her legs burned with each stride, and when she finally arrived she was quivering so much—from exertion, from adrenaline, from anticipation—that she tipped over sideways and gasped. She forced herself to look. *The red thing. What is it?* She popped off her skis, turned over, and began to dig around it, scraping quickly with her gloves. The snow had softened since yesterday, and she moved away a large scoop with her forearms, revealing the object.

A ski. Its red tip poked through, and when Julie dug

down around it she was able to pull it out. It was only twelve inches long at best, shattered, leaving an edge that looked like a row of broken teeth. Dylan's ski.

The rage vanished. "I'm sorry! I'm so sorry!" Julie fell back with a terrible howl, clutching the piece to her chest as her face melted with tears.

MATT

Location: Unknown river
Elevation: 9,000 feet

Leah grabbed him from behind, jerking his backpack toward her, but the bear had already closed the gap when it bolted into the space between them and her cub. They were hemmed in against the narrow rocky bank and the river.

Matt stumbled against Leah, shoving her sideways as he slipped out of his pack. He didn't know anything about bears, except the obvious. It was pissed. It was huge. And it was a mother defending its baby. He swung the pack in front of his chest as the bear let out a horrific bawl. The sound was like a something from a storm. It had a force and shape all its own, surrounding him like a hurricane wind. Then it passed through, an invisible wave that curled his toes and sent sparks shooting up his spine. He could have sworn his hair blew back.

The bear charged, stopping only ten feet away. Matt didn't move. He couldn't. His legs were stuck, rooted to the ground as if he'd been permanently planted. Carter had said something about this, but for the life of him Matt couldn't recall it. He was supposed to do something. *Or maybe I'm supposed to do nothing.* He pressed back against Leah, who didn't budge.

"Stop," she whispered.

"Stop what?" Matt croaked. The bear was so close he could smell it, and he couldn't understand how such a large animal could move like a racehorse out of a starting gate. Faster than what seemed possible. Definitely faster than him.

"There's nowhere left to go." Leah had her back against a fallen pine tree that had broken into two pieces across the water. It was chest high, with two feet of clearance underneath.

"Go over it!" Matt gasped. "Or under it. Just go!"

"Don't yell."

"I'm not!"

Too late. The bear charged again, a barreling hulk of fur and teeth and claws. Instinctively, Matt threw his pack, deciding as he launched it forward that it may have been one of the stupidest things he'd ever done. He only hoped it wouldn't be the last stupid thing.

When it hit the bear it bounced away like a rubber ball ricocheting off a brick wall.

But it worked, sort of. The bear stopped and shook its huge head, momentarily forgetting them. Curious, it went after the pack, swatting it with an enormous paw.

The snarl turned into a huff, and with one sharp swipe the pack ripped open, quick and easy down the zippered seam as though the bear had done this before. It stuck its face inside.

"Go," Matt whispered. "Go now."

Even after Leah heaved herself over the timber, Matt had a hard time moving. The bear snuffed and clawed at the nylon, strewing clothes and supplies on the rocks. When it found the beer it bit right into the can, sending a white spray of foam in his direction. He imagined the bear biting in his head like that, and figured his skull would crack as easily as the can—his cue to leave.

Only turning to check his footing, Matt managed to haul himself over the log. The bear didn't notice—too busy with the beef jerky and trail mix.

"There's another log downstream," Leah said quietly. "It's fallen completely across the river. I think it'll work as a bridge." She stared past him at the bear. The cub had scooted out from the bushes and was sniffing the now-empty beer can. "I don't think it will follow us."

"I hope you're right." Crunching noises. Shredding sounds. Snuffling grunts. When he peeked over the log, the bear raised its horribly large head and snarled, remnants of the beef jerky dangling from its snout. Matt knew the log between them wouldn't stop it, not by a long shot.

He turned and slid into a crouching walk, moving as fast as he could without running. Leah was already a good ten yards downstream, scrambling onto another wider timber. She was right; it had fallen almost exactly like a bridge across the water. Here the river was narrower, water rushing all the faster. And on the opposite side, where the limb was a few feet short of reaching the bank, was a small rock face—a short three-foot vertical rise. They'd have to jump. Matt saw it was still covered with snow—a shaded spot the sun never hit.

The log was spongy under his hands, cold and furred with army green moss. Matt pushed down twice, testing his weight, but a sudden roar behind him sprung him forward, and he came down hard, crotching it. "Ugh!" He knew it would hurt like hell in two seconds, but he didn't wait to feel it. The smell was suddenly on him, behind him. *Her.* The she-bear. A muggy, tangy smell of animal fur and mud with a sour garbage stench of breath. He crawled forward, inching like a worm. He squeezed his knees and ankles around the log, but after a few feet toward the middle his right foot slipped and fell down in the water. Instantly his leg was pulled under the log, and the sensation was not unlike a burn or an electric shock. He gasped, jerking his leg back in reflex, and almost tipped over to the other side.

He scooched forward a few more feet before he dared look back. The bear, now with its front paws up on the timber, watched him, tiny amber eyes glittering with interest and frustration. The log was too narrow for it to walk across. As he stared back, the long, slavering tongue rolled out of its mouth like an unfurling flag. The bear licked its muzzle, panted, and took a step into the water, never once taking its eyes off him. The current surged to its chest. If the water was too cold for the bear, it didn't show it.

Oh my God, he thought. *She's going to swim out here and rip me open like that bag of beef jerky.* He didn't wait to see what the bear would do next, but humped forward on his butt, hugging the limb with his thighs until he reached the middle.

"Matt! C'mon!" Leah was poised at the edge of the timber, like a frog squatting on her hands and feet, ready to spring to the rock wall.

"Leah, wait for . . ."

She jumped.

Me.

The log bounced, rolling sideways as she vaulted off, and he lurched back, overcorrecting as his gloved fist punched the surface. When he managed to pull himself back upright, Leah was clinging to the rock like a bug.

She made it.

But when she reached up, her right boot slipped. Her fingers missed the handhold.

Shit!

Leah hit the water with a loud splash. Her red hair swirled in the foam momentarily before disappearing under the surface.

"Leah!" Matt saw her coat, then her head and arms rise, but the current rushed her past the log, spinning her sideways underneath the branches. He swiped his hand as she flew past, but he was too far to reach her. "Leah!" Flashes of red, blue, and green; she came up spluttering, hair plastered across her mouth, then dunked under again. *Her pack!* Matt swiveled frantically on his seat as she clawed at the surface. *Her pack is pulling her down.* He needed to get off the log if he was going to accomplish anything useful.

He pushed up to standing, running down the rest of the log like a lumberjack, jumping the split second he felt himself begin to slide. It was a good leap and the rocks were slick with damp, but he jumped high enough that his chest cleared the top of the bank. He threw himself forward hard, looking for anything to grab. He heard another angry bawl as he landed, his eyes flicking back once to see the bear where he'd just been, paws up on the timber. It snorted once, as if in disgust, and retreated back to its cub.

Immediately he swung his legs around, rolling onto the snow, then popped up to his feet. Downstream he ran a twisting route around bushes and rocks, glancing at the rapids through the trees. Leah was stuck. He rounded an icy curve near the bank. Leah's hands clawed at something he couldn't see. He skidded down the bank, sitting down hard on a slick patch. He knew if he could find a spot near the water, he could haul her out.

"Leah, hang on!" Her head was tilted back in the river, face ice pale, eyes wide and staring. She gulped her mouth like a fish, while an unending flood of water poured over it, choking her. She was trapped, and she would drown soon if he didn't get her out. Matt forgot to care about the bear, or whether it cared about him. He forgot everything but Leah's face.

In two jumps he was down on the rocks, and he dropped onto his hands and knees. She was a few feet off the shore. The water wasn't deep—not more than chest high—but she was caught, stuck against a large boulder. He grabbed her shoulder and pulled. Leah screamed, "My foot! My boot! I can't pull it free!"

"Can you turn it?" Matt asked, trying not to panic. "Wiggle it free?"

"I . . . I c-can't even feel it anymore." Her lips were bloodless, stitched blue on the edges. "I can b-barely m-move."

Matt considered his options. And it became instantly clear he had just one: Get her free.

If he didn't, she'd die.

Failure wasn't an option.

He didn't want to remove his arm—it did a good job diverting the current, but already it was going numb. He couldn't help her like this. "Take a deep breath," he said. "I'll fix this."

She nodded and took a few shuddering gasps. Her eyes were dark as ink, turning glassy and clouding up like marbles. *I don't have much time.*

He scanned the shoreline, finally locating something he could use. "Okay, hold your breath. Now!" He removed his arm; the current rushed in against her face. He pushed back and sprinted a few yards upstream. A blackened branch stuck out of the swirling eddy, and he pulled it free, satisfied to see it was big enough to do the job.

He propped it back in front of Leah's face, next to her cheek. "Here. Can you hold this?"

"Yes," she spluttered, then took a welcoming breath, holding it tight with her right hand. "Hurry, Matt."

"I will." He pulled off his jacket, knowing what he needed to do, but suddenly questioning how or if he could. *This is going to hurt.* He stripped off his flannel, then his thermal shirt, kicking off his boots and pants as quickly as possible, until he was dressed only in boxers and his wool socks. Those he couldn't remove—something about trying this in bare feet was just too horrifying. And going commando would be too embarrassing. Matt still had enough self-consciousness left to consider the effect of ice cold water on his groin.

With gritted teeth he stepped in. First one leg, then the other, exhaling a stream of *shits* as the water rose over his thighs. *Shitshitshitshitshitshitshitshit.* Everything hurt, but he had to take it, take it and put it away. He had a job to do.

Inching in small movements toward Leah, he felt the rocks and pebbles and debris under his socked feet. He grabbed her shoulders, trying not to pass out in agony. "Wh-which leg is stuck?" He almost bit through his tongue, he shook so hard.

"Left."

The near side. He ran his hand down, trying to ignore the icy blast of water striking the side of his head, so cold it burned, as if someone had smacked him with a sizzling frying pan. A small explosion detonated inside his eardrum, leaving it ringing. Down, down, down past her kneecap, her shin, and now he knew he had to go under to reach her ankle. By this time, he was hyperventilating, but he plunged his head under, eyes shut, feeling all the way to the suede of her boot. His fingers found the grommets and laces and then the section of her arch where it was wedged into a perfectly foot-shaped crack at the bottom of the rock. He tugged. Nothing, not even a wiggle. His fingers throbbed. He couldn't hold it anymore; his air was gone.

"Dammit!" He sprayed at the surface. "It's really stuck in there!"

Leah coughed. "N-no s-shit."

Already she'd been in the water for five minutes, maybe closer to ten. He had to get her out soon or it would be too late. Drowning, he now understood, was no longer the problem.

All her clothes. All her stuff was wet. He pulled the pack off her shoulders and tossed it onto the bank, giving him a bit more room to maneuver. "Let me try something else." Another gulp of air and he went back down, this time forcing himself to keep his eyes open. It hurt like hell. Grit, sand, dirt, leaves whirled around him, up his nose and in his mouth, but he could see a little, enough to make out the metal grommets sparkling like small silver coins in the dim water.

If he could unlace the boot, she could pull her foot free. The laces were double tied and soaked through, but miraculously he pulled the right lace, releasing the knot. His fingers fumbled, clumsy and dense with cold, but he loosened the laces, unwinding them from the metal side hooks. It was done.

He came up gasping. "Can you wiggle it now? I unlaced it!"

"I . . ." Leah's eyes rolled back in her head like a broken doll's. "Am I? I c-can't f-feel . . ."

"Leah!" He was losing her.

He dived down again and grabbed her shin, then her ankle, and gave it one hard, wrenching twist, deciding it was better to have a broken foot than a dead body. He shook it, turned it, but found he did not have much leverage in the water. His body kept rising. He pulled her sock, making more space to pivot her foot. An inch was all he needed. Half an inch. A centimeter. Something. Another jerk. Her heel slipped up, popping out the back of her boot, and then the rest followed. When he resurfaced holding the boot, Leah was floating on her back, staring wide-eyed into the cloudy sky.

She had been in the water too long. Way too long.

With hands stiff with cold he managed to pull her out and up the shore. "Leah! C'mon! Walk!" He had to get her into dry clothes. "I need to get you out of this," he explained stupidly, tugging off her sopping wet jacket. Her pack was soaked through, along with everything in it. "I'll put you in my clothes."

Great idea, Matt. He shook his head. *What the hell are you going to wear?*

He did have a change of clothes, plus extra, in his pack, which meant he'd have to go back across the river, which meant he had to go back to the bear.

"Leah? Can you help me here?" It was like trying to undress a giant, shifting bag of potatoes. Finally, he peeled away her sodden hooded sweatshirt, then thermal shirt. Underneath was a hot pink tank top with small print scrawled across her chest. He looked closer at the sentence: *Stop staring at my tits!* He almost laughed, but he was shivering so hard it sounded more like a cackle. Black sports bra underneath that, and Matt's cheeks were now the only warm thing on his body—his groin still frozen numb. Eventually he got it all off, then put his clothes on her as quickly as possible. She never spoke, but Matt heard the constant clicking her teeth made.

"Leah, I need you to help me." He sat her down and began to remove her socks, before he realized his were soaking wet as well. "I have to go back for my pack." He squeezed her feet between his hands. "I have more dry stuff. We're gonna need it." He hoped the bear hadn't also eaten his clothes or ripped them to shreds in a fit of rage.

She nodded, glassy eyed, and he had no clue for the treatment of hypothermia other than what he was doing now. Dry clothes. Get her warm. Maybe he could make a fire, but he didn't have matches or a lighter, and even if he did, he doubted there was any dry wood. Everything was going from bad to worse to futile right in front of him.

But first things first. *Get the pack*, he thought, gritting his teeth. *Then go from there.*

His feet ached, toes cramped into painful curls that refused to straighten. He stripped off his wet socks, wrung them out, then forced himself to stuff his bare feet into his Merrells. Compared to the icy ground, the warmth of the boots was so amazing he almost cried. What was it the Buddhists say? Happiness is only the absence of suffering? That sounded about right.

Leah was sitting cross-legged on the ground, attempting to get out of the rest of her wet clothes. Matt took her movement as a good sign. And he really, really needed a good sign right now.

"Put these on." He handed her his corduroys. "They're big but they're dry." He turned away to give her privacy, and stared down into the gloom on the opposite bank where the bear had been but saw nothing. "I'm going to get the rest of my stuff. Be right back."

He thought he must have looked insane. He was almost completely naked, crawling across a log over a river. But he hoped he looked just crazy enough to frighten away whatever might be watching him from the trees.

For whatever reason, going across the log was much easier and faster the second time. When he landed on the opposite bank, he slid off the log, dropping into a wary squat. He kept his eyes on the bushes. The bear could be hiding back there with its cub, ready to charge him again. But Matt didn't have time to be cautious.

Scattered in the dirt twenty feet away, he saw his ripped-open pack, reflective piping glowing in the shadows. He crept forward, his heart pounding so loud in his ears it even drowned out the sound of the river. Stuff was everywhere. He gathered his dirty clothes, and then crunched something with his boot. Beer cans—punctured open and completely drained. Same for everything else that was edible. Every scrap of food was gone, leaving only plastic slivers of packaging.

Hurriedly, he pulled on a long-sleeve T-shirt, another plaid flannel, and topped it with a sweatshirt. He replaced his soaked boxers with a previously worn pair, as well as two pairs of used socks and the sweatpants he'd slept in the previous night. Then his dark gray polar fleece zip-up, an extra hat, and set of gloves. He was wearing almost everything he had, and he scavenged around for anything else he could see, quickly stuffing it back in the pack. Though the bag was scarred with claw marks and smeared with bear spit, the zipper still closed.

He checked the ground one more time, looking for anything useful he might have missed. There was a bit of garbage on the ground, and he realized if someone saw it they might figure out they had been here. It gave Matt an idea. He quickly went to work arranging the trash in a design, knowing it had to look intentional. A few minutes later he'd crafted a crude-looking arrow out of dented beer cans, plastic jerky packaging, and several foil scraps that remained from the Twix bar. Then he quickly crawled over the river a third time. He knew they wouldn't be able to travel right now, especially not in the condition they were in.

"Leah?" He inched along the bank, trying not to trip. "Where are you?"

No answer.

Farther down, he made out a shaking lump. She hadn't moved from the spot where he'd left her, and he grabbed her wet pack and lifted her up by her armpits. She shook so violently he could barely guide her up the bank. "We've got to get you warm," he said quietly. "We need to find shelter."

He debated making an igloo, but there was not nearly as much snow here. Less than a foot on the ground, bare in many spots, and no deep drifts to speak of. He guided her to a large, dark shape. Another huge pine tree, dead and rotting on the ground. It would make a good wall, and he looked around for more branches. "Sit here." Her wet hair felt crunchy. *Doesn't most heat leave the body through the head?* Matt put his fleece hat on her, pulling it down over her ears. What was that saying? *Head. Torso. Hands. Feet.* He put the extra set of gloves on her, then dug around for another pair of socks, putting the least scuzzy ones on her feet. He didn't put her boots back on; they were soaked.

Instead he used his own; he put on his sport sandals. He hadn't remembered to take them out of his pack the day before, and now was thankful he hadn't.

Matt turned Leah's wet boots upside down, propping them at an angle to dry. "Can you warm yourself up?" he asked. "Do some jumping jacks?"

She didn't seem to hear him, but gaped blankly at the dark woods, shivering.

He went through her supplies, which were mostly wet clothes, and pulled out the tarp and rope, trying to engineer a tent. *Sid would know how to do that,* he thought. But Sid wasn't here. He did find matches, but they were soggy and useless. There was a pair of snowshoes and he put those on, jerry-rigging the straps so they'd stay put around his sandals.

"Try to keep moving," he told her. "I'm going to build a shelter."

TONY

Location: Tent at abandoned NFS cabin,
Arapaho National Forest
Elevation: 9,000 feet

"Hurry!" Tony sprinted uphill, hit a deep drift, and collapsed forward, only to pop back up to greet the rescue team, which consisted of a lone skier coming down through the trees much too slowly for Tony's liking. "We're here! Hurry!" he barked.

And then he was there, towing a long sled behind him. "How many in the party?" The man removed his ski mask and exhaled a controlled breath.

"Four! No! Three!"

"Let's try again," the man replied in a calm voice, examining Tony as if he was a new psychiatric patient. "How many are here?"

"Three! One badly hurt. Chest injury."

The man barely reacted, only wiping at the crystallizing frost on his dark beard, then unhitched himself from the sled. It was bright orange, like a life raft, with black nylon straps crisscrossed on the top. "Where is he?"

"This way!" Tony flapped his arms like a frightened goose, but in reality he was relieved. Holding it together through all the hours of the night had taken their effect, and now the panic was finally coming out. Sid had stopped breathing for only a few seconds, but then the subsequent knowledge that Julie had left (with Carter's phone no less) had nearly sent Tony over the edge of reason. He didn't dare dwell on what might have happened if he hadn't checked on Sid when he did. As it was, Tony had done mouth-to-mouth resuscitation breaths, checking Sid's pulse after every third one. It remained, but faint, and Carter explained that he'd have to do chest compressions if Sid's pulse disappeared, which would have resulted in more broken ribs in the best-case scenario. The worst would be Carter accidently killing him.

After the longest, most excruciating minute of Tony's life, Sid resumed his whispery breaths, and Tony knew the rescue crew hadn't arrived a moment too soon.

The man crouched over Sid, taking a quick inventory, then looked up at Tony. His eyes were dark, at the same time bright and piercing like a bird's. "What happened, exactly?"

"He hit a tree." Tony twisted his hat in his hands; he didn't like the look the man was giving him. Too serious. *Dead serious,* thought Tony. "There was an avalanche." He stopped speaking then, too nauseated to explain what had become of Dylan. He hadn't really let himself think about it until now. Death had never been something to think about. Who was he kidding? In seventeen years he'd thought of it once—the time he flew off the swings and landed flat on his back, the oxygen blowing out of his lungs with such force that the pain made him unable to cry out. All he could do was gasp like a fish on the ground, and he wondered if Sid felt that now. If he had felt it all night. Now death was like a headache that refused to fade. It grew inside his head like a tumor, clinging to every thought and idea.

"We saw the slide when we flew over." The man nodded at Carter, who wore a stricken look, as if in physical pain. "You two okay?"

Carter opened his mouth, but Tony cut him off. "Yeah, we're both okay."

"Good." The man pulled out a walkie-talkie from a side pocket. "I'll let Ryan, the pilot, know. The Bell's parked up above the tree line. About a mile up."

"The Bell?" Tony asked.

"Bell 407. Helicopter." He removed a bright red sack from the sled. "I need you two to help me with this vacuum splint." He unfolded it; it looked to Tony like some sort of sleeping bag. "We'll get him on this and get him immobilized."

"Sid," Tony said reflexively. "His name's Sid. He's my brother. I'm Tony. That's Carter."

"I'm Will," the man replied as he spread the bag out on

the ground. "Okay, Tony and Carter, we'll do this on the count of three, all right?"

"Got it." Tony watched Sid. His brother's eyes were closed, mouth slightly open, and Tony tried to ignore the fact that he resembled a corpse, or that he could become one if they didn't get him out of there. Tony squatted down, positioning himself with his hands around Sid's ankles. Carter did the same with his shoulders. "I'm ready."

They helped Will carefully slid Sid onto the bag. Will pulled open a valve on the bag's side, inflating it. The red nylon puffed like a balloon around Sid, molding to his body.

"It's like a giant bean bag," Will explained, moving quickly as the bag solidified. Tony couldn't help but admire the calmness exuding from Will. Will didn't stutter, or hesitate, or panic, or raise his voice. He worked deliberately, tightening the nylon straps with a physical efficiency that was almost robotic. No movement wasted. "It will also help keep him warm. He needs to be off the snow."

"We had him in the tent last night," Carter said. "On a cot."

"Good thinking." Will nodded. "Okay, let's move him onto the sled."

When they lifted Sid again it was much easier, and Will helped them place him properly on the sled. "Now we have to ski back up," he said, attaching a towline to a carabiner on his belt. "I hope you guys have enough energy left."

"What about Julie?" Carter asked. "We can't leave without her!"

"Who?" Will turned around, stared at them dispassionately, checking them over as if doing a head count. "I thought you said three."

"We had four," Tony said, suddenly angry that Carter was wasting time. "Actually, we had seven."

"What?" Will was incredulous. "Where are they?"

"Dylan was the one buried in the avalanche," Carter explained. "Matt and Leah left to call for help. My sister Leah?" He looked sick at the mention of her name. "Did you got their call?"

"Yes, we got a call." Will considered this, looking hard at Tony. "Are they still out there?"

"I don't know," Tony admitted, flustered at the idea that Matt and Leah hadn't been found. They had apparently gotten the call through. Why hadn't they made it back? "Didn't you see them from the air?"

"It's hard to find people out here. Especially if they're in the woods," Will said. "And this Julie. Why did she leave this morning?"

"She didn't want to wait for help, I guess," Tony said. He wasn't about to try to explain the fight.

"Shit fuck," Will breathed. He shook his head at Tony. "Okay, here's what's going to happen." He pulled his ski mask down and grabbed his poles. "Your brother needs to be in a hospital, on the operating table. And he needed to be there yesterday." He tugged the towline as he started forward. "The ground crew already started searching a few hours ago, so I'll let them know about her. They'll have a good idea of where to look."

"We can't leave her out here!" Carter protested. He seemed surprised by Tony's indifference. "What's the matter with you?" he yelled at Tony.

"What's the matter with me? Nothing! I didn't leave!"

"What did you say to her?" Carter's green eyes sparked.

"Nothing! I didn't say a damn thing! I was sleeping!" Tony shot back. "Besides, she took your phone!"

Carter ignored that information. "Julie!" he screamed. "Where are you?"

"Let's calm down," Will commanded. "I need your help with this, all right?" He didn't wait for their answer, but started the long, arduous climb back up the mountain. "They are searching the area east of Berthoud Pass even as we speak. They have snowmobiles and hikers, a whole search party out there. Your friend Julie's on her own for now."

"I'll stay back and wait for her," Carter argued. "Why she left . . ." Carter cleared his throat. "I . . . I'm part to blame. I have to wait for her!"

"No way!" Will was firm. "I'm not leaving you here."

"Carter," Tony pleaded. "We can't stay. I can't stay. Julie will be fine for a few hours. Really."

Carter turned away, his shoulders shook for a few seconds, but then he straightened up, resigned. He nodded, wiped his eyes, and took his spot next to the sled.

"All right," Will said. "Now, let's move!"

MATT
Location: Crude shelter,
southeast of unknown river
Elevation: 9,000 feet

Matt had never built anything in his life, except maybe for
Lego sets. A castle. A fire station. The Millennium Falcon.
But he'd always followed the instructions, never deviating
or getting creative. But he was going to have to get creative
now. He tromped some distance away in the snowshoes,
eyes out for decent-size branches and rocks. He worked fast,
but was awkward in the snowshoes and his bare fingers were
clumsy with cold. He knew it was bad when he smashed his
thumb with the edge of a rock, but only noticed the injury
when a dark smear of blood appeared on his palm. He jogged
back and forth, collecting as much as he could carry, using
the rocks as a base support for the biggest branches, which
he stood upright like tent poles. He packed the wet snow
around them to cement them in place. Finished with the
frame, he ran the length of rope around the poles to make a
lopsided rectangle, and using the back of the fallen log as a

wall, he draped the tarp over. It was wide and long enough to reach the ground on the other side.

It was small, but big enough. After he unrolled his sleeping bag under the tarp, he helped Leah crawl in, pulling his pack behind him to block the opening. Already, it was warmer.

"Feeling better?" Matt asked. They were packed in tight and despite his numb feet and face, he was almost on the verge of breaking a sweat. But his hands were wretched, bloody, and practically paralyzed. He tucked them under his sweatshirt and shuddered. His fingers felt like ice cubes against the heat of his stomach.

Leah trembled, still silent, so Matt touched her face with his hands, not feeling any difference in temperature. She kept her eyes squinted shut, then suddenly muttered, "Don't."

"Leah?"

"D-d-don't t-t-touch me." A violent spasm vibrated through her, like she was being electrocuted, jerking her arms and legs. Her feet kicked his shins. Her fists punched his face.

"Ow! Stop!"

"Don't!"

"It's okay!" he yelled, which was the opposite of being okay, but he didn't know what else to say. "It's okay! I won't touch you."

Her eyes opened—a small whine hummed in her throat as she balled her fists under her chin.

"You might have hypothermia," he said slowly, hoping she understood and didn't try to punch his teeth in. He didn't need to lose another one. "It can make you get weird." He didn't really know this, but Leah was acting like someone having a really bad drug-induced fit.

"W-where's Sid?"

"He's with Tony and Carter, remember?"

"Carter!" Her voice cracked. "I w-want Carter!"

"Carter's not here," he said, trying to soothe her. "I'm here. It's me. Matt. I'm trying to help you."

"F-f-fuck off."

She was obviously delirious. He couldn't see her face in the dark, but heard the tears in her voice. And the panic. "Okay." He tried to think of something else that might calm her down. "Are you hungry?"

That was probably the stupidest question he'd ever asked—so stupid Leah didn't answer. Suddenly feeling witless, Matt began to babble, talking as if his life depended on it. Maybe it did. He needed to distract her from the cold. He needed to distract himself. *Food,* he thought. It always seemed to come back to food. "Well, I'm hungry. I'm *starving*. Back at home in Des Moines, I used to go to this restaurant called Goobers. They had the best cheeseburgers ever. Thick quarter pounders. Fresh Angus beef. I always ordered mine with bacon. And it wasn't this skinny little crap bacon either, but the good stuff. Thick-cut pepper bacon. Applewood smoked. Extra onions. Sharp cheddar cheese. Homemade buns. I think they were called brioche or something. They buttered and grilled them." His mouth puddled with saliva on *butter*. "And the french fries. Oh my God. Just the best french fries in the universe. Crispy. Salty. Steaming hot. But I never dipped mine in ketchup," he continued. "I hate ketchup. I dipped them in my chocolate malt. Salty fries and chocolate ice cream." He could easily picture the table in front of him, hot and waiting for him, like a centerfold porno of food, and he vaguely wondered if talking about it at a time like this constituted a version of torture. Probably.

"K-k-ketchup?" Leah interrupted, shuddering the word like a curse.

"Huh?"

"W-who the h-h-hell doesn't like k-ketchup?"

"Me," he answered, hoping this meant she wasn't going to punch him in the face again. "I hate it. It's disgusting."

"D-d-do you h-hate tomatoes?"

"No."

"V-vinegar?"

"No."

"Sh-shugar? Salt?"

"No."

"Tha-that's k-ketchup," she blurted triumphantly, as if to prove some point he wasn't aware of.

"I know what ketchup is."

"Th-then yuh-yer w-weird."

"I'm weird?"

She was quiet for a second, trembling against him in such a way that he realized his groin wasn't as frozen dead as he thought. Things below the belt started to stir. His pulse rose from a half to four-four time. "Wha-what about mu-mu-mustard?"

He exhaled slowly, trying to turn his mind back to food. "I don't like mustard either."

"B-b-but there's a h-hundred ka-kinds."

"So?"

"De-Dijon m-mustard?"

"Nope."

"You ever t-try it?"

"No."

When she answered again, he heard the smile in her voice. "Then y-you d-don't know t-till you t-try."

"My mom says that," he replied immediately. "But I don't agree. Maybe I don't know what I like, but I'm pretty sure about what I don't."

"Nuh-uh. Y-your m-mom s-sounds-s-smart."

"Yeah," he had to admit. "She is." He suddenly thought of her, wondered what she was doing at this exact moment. It was evening; she might be watching the news, maybe she was even waiting for him to call, not being able to go to sleep until he checked in. She'd always been like that, needing reassurance from him that he would be fine but never believing him until she got confirmation, and he wondered if that was how all mothers were. Or was it just his? And now he could see why she did worry; he could see how she believed something innocent and fun could turn on a dime. How things could change in an instant. Because they had. "My mom is probably wondering what I'm doing right now."

"C-camping?"

Even Matt had to laugh. "This is the worst camping trip I've ever been on."

"The t-tent is n-n-not so h-hot either."

She was making jokes; that was a good sign. "Yeah, maybe I should update my Facebook post. *Having a great time in Colorado! Enjoying nature and the wildlife!*"

She pressed closer against him, convulsing with laughter, and he had the desperate urge to put his arms around her, and not just to keep her warm. "F-Facebook is s-s-stupid."

"That's what everyone says." He rested his hand on her shoulder, needing to touch her, if only a little. "But everyone's on it."

"N-not me."

"Really?" Now he was surprised. "I thought every female was on Facebook. Or at least Instagram. Twenty selfies a day." He knew people who did this—most of them girls in his high school. Posing with that same acidic look—tilted chin, angling for a mood crossed between bored, sly, and pissed off, a calculated gaze bordering on confusion.

"G-guys d-do it t-t-too," Leah stuttered, still shaking. He needed to keep her talking, keep her awake, and keep his mind off her body, which was downright impossible.

He'd never been this close to a girl before, and though he had imagined more than a hundred times (maybe closer to a thousand) what it would be like to actually get naked with one, he could honestly say he'd never imagined this particular scenario.

"I guess so." Matt discerned that there was a certain subset of people who didn't have profiles on the Internet. Types of people you just couldn't find. And as far as he knew, he could think of six.

1. Old people who thought the interwebs were something to do with technologically advanced spiders.

2. Prison inmates or mental patients (although they might get computer privileges).

3. Criminals hiding from the police and/or mafia.

4. Undercover agents working for the police and/or mafia.

5. People who lived in third world countries with no access and/or people who didn't own a computer.

6. People who had a secret and didn't want to be found.

Out of these six options, Matt thought only numbers three and six could be true, and he highly doubted a person could be much of a criminal or police informant by the ripe old age of seventeen.

So he went with number six.

"Leah?"

Quiet.

"Leah, wake up."

"N-no," she murmured. "I'm tired. I need to sleep." At least she had almost stopped shaking, but he was suddenly afraid that was a bad thing.

His hand slid down, dropping from her shoulder to the soft curve of her stomach. He pulled her toward him and she curled into him with a soft sigh. "I don't want you to fall asleep," he whispered into her hair. She smelled like the river, fresh and bright and cold and a scent that made him think of the color green. Green. She smelled *green*.

"I have to. S-so do you."

"I know." Fatigue settled in his bones like a lead weight; it was now painful to keep his eyes open. "How do you feel?"

"Like sh-shit," she mumbled. "Like I almost d-drowned in a r-river."

"True."

"Th-thank you, by the way."

"Well, I owed you one."

"Yeah. M-maybe." More quiet. "I g-guess we're even."

That was a weird way of putting it, Matt thought, but it made him feel better. Not as useless and annoying as he did this morning. "I've never met a girl like you," he professed into the dark. Who was he kidding? He'd never met anyone, male or female, like her before.

"Is that g-good?"

"Yeah. Definitely."

"Thanks."

She was quiet then, breathing softly, evenly, and he wondered why it was easier to say what he thought now, although this small, dark space did resemble a confessional booth.

Leah's breathing was soft and wispy, her body snug against his own, and he pulled the extra flap of sleeping bag over them. He didn't know how long they'd been lying there; his thoughts ran on and time seemed to lose meaning. But he knew he couldn't stay awake all night listening for her breath, checking for her heartbeat.

"Please don't die," he whispered. Matt closed his eyes and thought about praying, but knew it didn't matter. It didn't matter what he believed, or if he believed anything at all. Based both on his limited experience and pure rational observation, he knew things didn't happen for a reason, there was no cosmic scorecard, no judgment day balance sheet, and that a lot of good people had horrible things happen to them, and bad people did sometimes get away with murder. Right now he could pray all he wanted. He could beg and bargain and plead. But it didn't matter. The universe didn't care about him any more than he cared about a grain of sand on a beach a thousand miles away. No one was listening.

He knew this.

But he still prayed.

He prayed because he was afraid of being alone.

"Don't die, Leah," he repeated with the fervor of a saint. "Don't die. Okay?"

"Okay," she finally mumbled back. "I won't." She slipped one hand into his (still cold but not as icy) and gave a determined squeeze.

He believed her; he had to believe in something. And so he tucked his chin down, pressing his face against her damp hair with a releasing breath, and waited to stop thinking, waited for things to shut down, go silent and blank.

Sometimes Matt thought falling asleep must be exactly like dying. You don't really notice it when it happens to you.

TONY

Location: Tent at abandoned NFS cabin,
Arapaho National Forest
Elevation: 9,000 feet

"Carter! C'mon! Let's go!"

Carter crouched over, hurriedly scribbling something on a piece of paper. At the last second he had decided he needed to leave a note for Julie. He ripped a sheet from a small notebook, folded it, and crawled into the tent, hoping she'd return and find it.

Dammit, Julie. Tony clenched his fists and grabbed the sled towline from Will, clipping it on the harness. *Why couldn't you just have waited a little longer?* Now Carter was freaking out and wasting time. Time they didn't have.

"Ready?" Will squared his shoulders. "Left, right, left, right," he coached Tony, and together they moved forward, back onto the trail Will had made coming down. Now it was all uphill. Tony took a steadying breath and leaned into the weight, not looking back. Carter could catch up.

Right, left, right, left. Tony staggered sideways on the incline.

"We just need some momentum," Will said. "A little faster and we'll smooth out."

"Okay," Tony huffed, wondering if this was how a sled dog felt. He poked the snow with his poles, matching his stride to Will's. "I think I got it."

"Good."

A few strides later the load lightened, and Tony glanced back. Carter, in his snowshoes, pushed doggedly at the rear of the sled. He had his skis crisscrossed and attached to his pack, and it looked like a more difficult job than the one Tony had.

"Good pace, guys. Steady on. We've got a thousand yards," Will said, eyes straight ahead. He pulled out a walkie-talkie from his side pocket without breaking stride. "I'll let Ryan know to call UCH and tell them we're coming."

"UCH?"

"University of Colorado. They have a helipad that can handle us." Will relayed a series of commands through the receiver, and the pilot responded through the static. Tony wondered what their conversation meant. A lot of tens were spoken. He guessed it was all walkie-talkie lingo. Will said things like, *ten-nine repeat, ten-twenty-five for UCH, ten-twenty-three stand by.* The volley went back and forth for a minute before Will uttered a final "ten-four." It was the only thing Tony understood. *Message received.*

"Does the pilot know? Did you tell him?" Carter panted. "He needs to know!"

"Yes." Will didn't slow down, but continued his relentless stride forward. "I let him know about your friend Julie. He'll radio the sheriff. Like I said, they're already out looking."

"And they'll find her? Can you tell them where to look?"

Tony didn't like the sound of Carter's voice; he wished Carter would just focus on the sled, which was difficult enough. Sid made little groans and gasps when the sled went over a bump or jerked sideways. *Good,* Tony thought. *He's still there.* Complaining was fine. And while Tony wanted to say the right thing to Carter so he would calm down, he didn't have a clue where to start. So he did the next best thing—he ignored him. "Do you guys work for the park service?" Tony asked Will, trying not to sound like he was going to faint. He'd never passed out before, and given their circumstances, couldn't afford to find out what it was like. "Like the rescue crew or something?" He pinched the bridge of his nose, trying to clear the throb in his temples. Sweat drenched his back. He wanted to stop and remove his coat, but that was more wasted time. *Ignore it. Keep going. Right, left, right, left.*

Will shook his head. "This isn't national park land. It's national forest."

"Oh." Tony didn't understand why that made a difference, though he remembered Dylan saying something about that the night of the party.

"The jurisdiction is Grand County."

"Oh."

"We're volunteers."

"Volunteers?" This time Tony did stop; his right foot slid so far forward he almost did the splits. Recovering, he jerked the harness with such force, he felt it in his throat. *These people volunteered to go out and search for us? To search through an avalanche? To risk their own lives? And it wasn't their job? They weren't getting paid?* He opened his mouth, trying to say the words, wanting to thank Will, wanting to fall down and cry, wanting to run and hide. *I'm so stupid,* Tony thought. *Stupid and careless.* Up until this point, Tony didn't imagine there were other people in the world who were much different from him. People who didn't always think about themselves. People like Will. Like Ryan the pilot. Like the strangers searching the woods for them right now. Knowledge was a hot, shameful flood inside him, filling straight up to his eyes.

If Will noticed Tony's tears he didn't mention it, but kept pulling forward, eyes looking ahead on the trail. "Well, I always thought this was more interesting than fishing."

Tony didn't know what to say to that either, but managed to nod.

"Thank you, Will," Carter said from the back.

"Yeah," Tony said softly. "Thank you."

Will bobbed his head in a quick nod, concentrating on the incline ahead. The snow was soft, sloppy, but the skins on the skis prevented them from backsliding. Every muscle in Tony's back and legs screamed, but he ignored it, putting his entire one-hundred-forty-five-pound frame into the climb. After what seemed like an hour of pulling, the incline flattened out.

"Great job!" Will did not slow down. In fact, he did the opposite, picking up speed. Tony had never seen another person with this kind of robotic strength. Will was not much bigger than him, but showed no signs of fatigue. There was a hardness about his physique, as if his arms and legs were made of steel cables and iron rebar. "We're close."

They skied around a wedge of evergreens and the helicopter came into view, red and white and glowing in the sun. And though Tony wasn't religious, his reaction to the sight was as if he were the most devout Catholic now beholding the face of the Virgin Mary. He fell to his knees in the snow and crossed himself.

The engine burr vibrated Tony's bones, and he watched the long blades whip the surrounding treetops into submission. The helicopter, starting up, sounding more like a jet engine progressively building into a supersonic scream. A few moments later he felt the dip and sway as it left the ground. Tony gripped Sid's hand, holding fast ever since Will and Ryan had loaded him on a stretcher, and watching the trees shrink away as they rose. The sight was so dizzying Tony had to focus on something else, something stationary. Puking here was not an option.

"How long?" he called, his voice barely audible above the engine. Both the pilot and Will had on headsets, communicating back and forth, but Tony couldn't guess the severity of their conversation. They also wore mirrored sunglasses, leaving their faces undecipherable.

Sid's face, in contrast, was drawn, his lips dry and slightly parted. His exhalations were as slight as an infant's. Dark, threadlike capillaries stood out like stains on his eyelids. "Hang on, Siddhanth," he whispered. "We're almost there."

The hospital was twenty minutes away, according to the pilot, and the sky was clear. They should have a fast flight. Carter sat opposite Tony, with his head pressed against the window, scanning the ground with restless eyes, his fists balled against his thighs in such a way that he reminded Tony of a jack-in-the-box, tightly wound and ready to pop.

When Tony looked out the window again he felt less ill. The helicopter was moving forward fast enough that the initial stomach-tilting sensation had left him. Sunlight gleamed off the snow, and Tony examined the terrain below. According to Will, Denver was a thirty-minute flight from their location. Thirty minutes to civilization. A half hour to hope. Tony guessed by the way the ground flew past them that they were going at least a hundred miles per hour, and he did a mental calculation on the possible distance. At least fifty miles. The mountains in the distance, however, seemed immobile.

A flash of red caught Tony's eye. It was a slight, quick thing. Just a dot in all that white. There and gone, and he leaned his head against the window and squinted. What was it? Just a fraction of something, but definitely red. Or was it pink? A color somewhat between the two, and Tony remembered the word. *Coral.* That was the color. Wasn't Julie wearing a coat that color? He couldn't remember, but it was something bright and pretty. Tony pressed his lips in a tight line. Sunlight bounced off the glass, and the sharp glare forced his eyes back to the interior. *Nothing,* Tony decided. *It was nothing. Just a trick of the light.* He squeezed Sid's hand, keeping perfectly silent, perfectly still. *They can't stop anyway. They can't even hear what I say.*

Across from him, Carter sat hunched over, his head bent to his chest, and he held himself still. Tony bent his head too, eyes on his brother's face, and swallowed hard.

He didn't see anything. Nothing at all.

Outside, a thin gray line took shape on the ground. Interstate 70 heading east into the city. The helicopter flew on.

JULIE

Location: Bills Peak, tree line
Elevation: 10,500 feet

Julie had been climbing steadily for some time, eager to reach a ridgeline and get a signal. The trees were thick on this slope, an army of pines and aspens that made it impossible to pick a straight route through. But Julie wasn't bothered; she was on a mission, and soon enough the foliage and air thinned. She was almost there, and she continued on, eating a banana with one hand while schussing through soft powder. She tossed her banana peel into a drift just as the helicopter appeared over the hill, zooming over her so fast with a crescendo and fade out that she didn't even have time to blink. The helicopter flew past her over the trees.

"No!" Julie screamed, realizing her mistake. *Which way? Which way was it going?* She'd been skiing several hours, and now she had no idea whether to return on the trail she'd left or continue on to the top. *Leah and Matt must have gotten the call through! They are searching!* Impulsively, she turned, deciding to return to Carter. She was a fast skier, and the way back was mostly downhill. If the helicopter was heading to the cabin, it would have to land somewhere. It might take them an hour or longer to complete an extraction. And if she hurried, she might make it. It was all downhill from here.

Renewed by confidence, she swooped down the hill, heading back to the cover of the trees. *Stay in the tracks,* she thought, and as she cut a path through the trees, a bright blur of gold flashed in the corner of her eye. Something was coming, and it was moving fast, much faster than she was.

The mountain lion struck her sideways, a T-bone collision, and it flung her over, cartwheeling onto her head. Steaming animal breath hit her face as it raked its claws across her back, thankfully protected by her pack and nylon parka. But the cat dug in, curling her into its grip with a tight feline hug, back legs thrusting at her like a spring-loaded device. Julie gasped, striking out with her pole, stabbing the point blindly until it made contact. The cat snarled and Julie screamed back as it leaped off, only now knowing what it was that had just attacked her.

"Stop! Dammit!" She stabbed both poles forward like fencing swords, but the mountain lion didn't run. "Back!" It flattened down into a rug before her, amber eyes boring into her own. "Back off! Now!"

Tail twitching like a serpent, it spat a hiss, revealing long yellow canine teeth. Julie stabbed once more with her pole; she was dangerously off balance on her skis, and she knew she couldn't allow it another chance to strike. The metal tip of the pole caught the cat's nose, and it screeched a horrible gut-chilling noise. Startled by the pain, the cat seemed to reconsider, and with another flick of its tail, it turned and bounded up the slope. But Julie didn't wait to see it go. She was already flying wildly down the hill, still screaming, still thinking the cat was coming for her, and in her panicked state she swung sharply right. Trees were everywhere. Branches caught her shoulders, smacked her arms and legs, everything threatening to knock her flat. Julie tucked herself together and bent her knees, picking up speed. She wasn't going to let it catch her. Not now. Not when she was so close. *Don't look back*, she thought. *Just keep going. Don't stop.* Another sharp curve came up and she cut it neatly, digging her edges in. *Faster. Go faster.* The woods opened up suddenly, blue sky everywhere. Above her. Below her. Everything was blue. Because in her haste, Julie had just launched herself straight off a cliff.

It was high. Over five hundred feet. Six hundred and thirty-seven feet, to be exact. Adrenaline was everywhere, flooding every synapse, snapping every nerve. Strange thoughts flickered in her mind as she shot out into the air, arcing up like a ski jumper. *An open window, pink gingham curtains fluttering in late afternoon sunlight. The thick slapping of flip-flops on hot pavement, a lime Popsicle melting sticky sugar down her chin, her hair streaming out behind her as her father pushed her on her new blue bicycle. The sun, the* mountains, the snow sparkles in front of her face whirled around her. She was still heading up, reaching the zenith of her path. *The tug and pull of an ocean wave, the salt in her mouth, her mother's dry cool hand on her forehead, the scent of her skin, lilac and basil and Ivory dish soap, lemon-yellow fireflies winking on and off in the dark blue evening as she chased her older sisters across the lawn, damp grass slick and cool between her toes.*

Julie's eyes were wide open now, seeing everything, and as she began her descent to Earth, she gasped. Not in fear, but in pure amazement. Pure wonder. Because as she watched the view spread out in front of her, all bright blue and white, with heaven and Earth indistinguishable, it turned into the best dream she'd ever had. A dream she never wanted to end. And for those few moments the dream was real.

She was flying. And it was beautiful.

DAY 4

THE HUNTER
Location: West of unknown river

By the time the sun was directly overhead, the cat had reached the river. The scent trail had been weak at first, but now it stood stock still between the aspens, eyes half shut, smelling. It was strong here. Recent and close. The cat moved with a long, pacing stride down the ravine, mouth open and breathing deeply. The river held little interest, but the animal stopped long enough to lap a quick mouthful of water. Satisfied, it continued on downstream, picking its way over rocks as smoothly as the river itself.

A few yards later it froze, scruff bristling to attention, and growled deep in its throat. A different smell was here, concealing the original. The cat snorted and backed away. Nervous, it leaped over the fallen timber, catching another whiff of the trail as it cleared the limb.

It circled back, confused. The cat would not climb the log; it would not cross the river. Not here. It stood quietly, examining the other bank.

The stink of bear was overpowering, so it moved down the bank, looking for a crossing. But the river was wild and raging here, and so it continued downstream, forced by insistent hunger. The last creature had startled it, just enough for it to get away, leaving the lion with a bloody mark on its muzzle. But the injury was nothing compared to its need to eat, and it would not give up so easily again. A few miles downstream there was a precipice of rock jutting out across the water—a twelve-foot jump to the other side. Which would not be a problem for the cat.

MATT
Location: Crude shelter,
southeast of unknown river
Elevation: 9,000 feet

It wasn't light that woke him, but sound. A cutting thud.
A mechanical whine. Matt reeled through his catalog of
common noises until his brain landed on a winner.

Helicopter. Chopper blades. The whupping beat grew
and then ebbed.

His eyes popped open, but everything was shadows,
dim outlines of gray and black. Was it the same helicopter
as before? Were they still looking? How could they fly
in the dark? With one hand he pushed the pack out the
opening—sunlight streamed in like a flood. *How long have
we been sleeping?*

He had built the shelter in the early afternoon—at
least, judging by the sky he'd thought so. They must have
slept straight through the night, and as he inched out from
underneath the tarp he saw the reason for his confusion.

Snow. At least a foot of new powder covered everything,

muffling every sound in the woods except for the one that woke him. The *whup, whup, whup* of blades faded overhead. Where was it? Here the trees were thick as carpet; he couldn't go running off into the snow even if he wasn't worried about getting lost. He was wearing only sandals.

"Leah!" He lifted the end of the tarp, carefully sifting off the snow. It was light and fluffy as talcum powder, not the heavy, wet cement that would have collapsed their tent. He cringed. *Don't even think about that.* Leah was curled up, hands tucked into her armpits, head barely visible from the coat. She was so still and pale that a flash of panic flared behind Matt's eyes. Spots and blobs of darkness crept into the corners of his vision. He opened his mouth, then shut it, terrified by what the truth might be.

But it was simple.

She was either alive or she wasn't.

He touched her hair, somehow believing the answer would be obvious when he made contact. But it wasn't. He wiggled her shoulder. "Leah, wake up." Pressing his palm onto her neck, he held his breath and counted to ten.

On eight she groaned and he released his hand. "What time is it?" Her voice was thick with sleep.

"Don't know. Morning, I think."

"Early?" she whispered.

"I heard a helicopter."

"When?" She raised her head out fully from the coat, like a turtle poking out of its shell. Dark purple shadows decorated the skin under her eyes, making her look like she'd been in a boxing match and lost. "Where?"

"Just now." He cocked his head, hearing only silence. He was positive he didn't imagine it.

She wiped her eyes, and Matt saw her fingers shake. "What direction did it go?"

"I don't know. I didn't see it."

"But you just said . . ."

"I said I heard one," he replied. "I did. Honest."

She didn't argue, but sat up and looked around her, disbelieving. "It snowed!"

"At least a foot, looks like."

"Shit."

"Why? Is that bad?"

"Well, it's not *good*." She pushed herself to a tilted stance, a bit too shaky for Matt's comfort. Hands on her hips, she surveyed the woods. "It'll be harder for them to see where the avalanche was, harder to spot the trail we made." She shook her head, red curls bouncing, the only lively looking thing about her. "Well, whatever trail we made is gone."

"I guess we'll have to make a new one." Matt found the clothes and boots where he'd set them out to dry, but now they were covered with snow and still wet, at least the boots were. The leather was so stiff it felt frozen; he doubted she'd be able to wear them. He was stuck with his sandals, but if he could layer on another pair of socks, and then wear the snowshoes, it might work. He hoped so; he didn't really have much of a choice. He clapped the boot soles together with a hollow *thump*. "How are you feeling this morning?"

"Like I have a hangover." Leah pinched the bridge of her nose between her thumb and forefinger. "Without the fun part the night before."

Matt nodded; he felt the same. Dry and gummy mouth, thick furred tongue, gritty eyes and aching head. *Everything* on his body ached, especially his toes, and he stamped his feet trying to get circulation going while looking for the snowshoes. He had set them next to the boots and he had to dig around with a stick before he found them. After he crammed on another pair of socks and strapped the snowshoes around his sandals, he looked up to see Leah's expression. Matt couldn't tell if she was in pain, frightened, or just annoyed.

"What's wrong?"

"You can't go walking around in that!" She glanced down at her boots, which were actually his. "You should put these back on." She sounded embarrassed, but she also looked like she'd rather jump back into the river than take them off. She shuffled unsteadily forward in the fresh snow toward him.

"I will," he said, holding her pair up, laces tied together in a fat wet knot. "As soon as these dry out we can switch."

"Well, then let me wear the snowshoes first."

"No, you need to keep your feet warm." Matt didn't want to tell her that he had been afraid she might die last night, that in some ways she looked as if she had, and now returned as a specter, some faded shadow of herself. *Death warmed over* was the expression Matt's mother used on occasion. *No,* thought Matt. *Not a good choice of words, no matter how accurate.*

"Okay," she said finally. "We'll switch off every mile."

He didn't ask how many miles she thought it would be. It might be easier if he didn't know. "I'm hungry." He didn't know why he bothered stating the obvious. There was no food. He folded up the tarp into a small square, then coiled the rope.

"Me too." Leah stared blankly at the trees. "I could go for some breakfast."

Breakfast. His stomach twisted on the word. Images of steaming buttermilk pancakes, shimmering with a glaze of butter and a cascade of maple syrup, flashed in his head. Sizzling peppered bacon, poached eggs that released their golden liquid yolks at the touch of a fork tine. Pork sausage links, plump and glistening with fat and spices. A mound of hash browns, crispy with burned edges. He could eat all that right now, plus a few chocolate-glazed doughnuts, and wash it down with strong black coffee.

He scooped up a handful of snow, forcing the mental food porno from his head. "I guess this is breakfast." He crunched it in the back of his mouth, and it dissolved like a chunk of cotton candy, minus the sugar.

"We just need to keep going down this way." Leah

took the tarp and rope and zipped them into her pack, then swung it on her shoulders. She stumbled sideways a few steps, looking a bit drunk, but Matt knew her pack was like his—mostly empty. They wore all the dry clothes they had left, and he wondered, given her condition, if he should offer to carry the pack. Immediately, he dismissed the idea. She'd never let him do that.

With a quick snap, Leah clipped the buckle around her waist and shortened the straps, tightening them around her like a cage, as if this would somehow help her stay upright. "We should hit something soon, especially if we keep heading down. Probably a road."

"Do you think the helicopter will come back?"

"Maybe." Leah glanced up at the sun, checking the position.

"Do you think they found them?"

"God, I hope so," she breathed, dropping her shoulders. "Then they'll know about us."

"I wish I had my phone." Matt bit down on his tongue, remembering why he didn't. Even if he did, the battery would be dead by now.

"Well," Leah said, "the bear probably would have eaten that too."

"Have you ever heard of these things happening out here before?"

By these things, he meant the following:

Avalanches. Mortal wounds. Hypothermia. Bear attacks. What else did he forget? What else was there?

Matt thought of Murphy's Law. *Whatever can go wrong, will.* That seemed to be true, and it was getting truer by the minute.

"I think these things happen all the time," Leah answered. "It's just that they've never happened to us." She started off, legs shuffling and hesitant, and to Matt she resembled a prisoner just released from a dungeon. Tired and shaky. Hopeful, yet wary. She squinted in the sunlight, slowly breaking a new trail through the snowfall. Matt followed.

They made strange tracks. Matt followed Leah's boot prints, high-stepping in the snowshoes in an attempt to keep his socks free of snow. It worked for a minute—the exact amount of time it took for his legs to start shaking. His gait descended to a plodding shuffle.

"That bad, huh?" Leah asked, her voice abnormally loud in the still morning. The snowfall had muted the landscape, and not just with a lack of color. The silence was a weight all its own, a muffled blanket on their backs.

"I'm already tired," he puffed. "And it's still early."

"We can switch. I can snowshoe for a stretch." She bent down and unlaced the boots.

"Okay." Matt thought she was in a pretty good mood, and he wondered if that was a consequence of coming so close to dying. She also looked better. The purple shadows under her eyes had faded to lavender. "You sound better," he offered as they traded footwear.

"I'd *be* better if I had some coffee and a plate of *huevos rancheros*," she said.

"Oh," he groaned, stomach twisting. "Yeah, let's not talk about that." He shoved his cramping feet into the Merrells. They were warm, but underneath his socks, on his right foot, his toes burned in a way that he'd only ever felt once before. He pressed them, wiggled them, trying to get the circulation going, but they felt as hard as pebbles. Not good.

"Okay, let's talk about you instead."

"Let's not." Matt cringed, tightening the laces over his forefoot. Maybe if he tied them tight his feet wouldn't ache so much. Or would it make it worse? "I'm not very interesting."

"Everyone's interesting if you really get to know them."

"Not me." Matt thought so far the only truly interesting thing that had happened to him was, in fact, happening right now. And if evading death as many times as he had in the past two days was interesting, he figured he was now the most fascinating person on the planet. "You seemed really out of it last night," he said, changing the subject. He decided loose boots were better than tight, and tied the laces lightly. He flexed his feet.

"I was," she admitted. "But I wasn't *that* out of it."

"I thought you might die." The word *die* came out of his mouth like a filthy curse—he twitched. "I thought you had hypothermia."

"I think I did, sort of. I mean . . . if I'd been alone . . ." She seemed to imagine this possibility in detail and shuddered. "Yeah, I would have been totally screwed."

"I didn't know what to do." A clump of snow fell off a high branch and plopped at the base of the tree. Already the sun was melting it. "And then I'd have been screwed."

"Well, you did just fine." Leah took her place behind him, and Matt stepped into smooth powder, careful to keep his stride short. She followed, hop-stepping in the snowshoes. "Something tells me you'd be okay."

"Oh yeah? What gives you that impression?"

"Years of experience." Leah laughed. It sounded like an old door creaking open.

"I'm not in the best shape," he admitted. "And I've almost bit it more than twice." He couldn't bring himself to say the word *die* again.

"But you didn't give up," Leah said. "That's why you made it. In the end, survival has to do with this." She tapped her temple with her finger. "At least, that's what Carter says."

"So it's all mental, then?" Matt didn't believe that. Not really. But he found he couldn't argue with it, either. Some people did survive purely because they believed they would. They made a choice to make it. But there were plenty of others who never even got the chance to choose.

"Mostly." She smiled as if his doubts were obvious on his face. "Being lucky doesn't hurt either."

Matt nodded. "It's better to be lucky than good."

"Who said that?"

"Not sure." Matt bit his lip. "But my dad says it all the time."

"You believe that?"

Tall spires of evergreens poked their tips into the blue sky. The sun was still shining and the sky was still blue. If he had a camera he'd take a picture, but all a photograph would show was snow and pines. Mountains and sky. An untouched wilderness. Pristine beauty. But underneath all that beauty was an unforgiving cruelty. Matt saw that now; it was like being able to see an underpainting on a masterpiece—the deeper layers becoming visible, rising to the surface, and he knew the truth. The wild was indifferent to his suffering; it would crush him like a bug. It could at any moment. Matt tilted his chin up, closing his eyes against the sun. "I do now."

They traveled for a mile through the snow-draped pines. His breathing came slower, deeper. It was easier to draw in the air he needed, despite all the work he did making the trail. They had definitely dropped to a lower elevation; he felt it in his chest and ears when he swallowed. "How high are we now?" Below his boots, the snow had shrunk to half its depth, and if the sun stayed it might be gone by the end of the day. This made him stop and eat scoops of slush until his teeth ached. Hungry was bad, but thirsty was worse. Way worse.

"Eight thousand feet?"

"That high still?" The trees were even thicker here, and

he doubted that if the helicopter did pass over, it would see them. They might have to hike all the way out. "How many more miles, you think?"

Leah sank down against a trunk. "I don't know." She unstrapped the snowshoes.

"What about the helicopter? Do you think it'll come back?"

"No." She shrugged and bent her head. "Yes. Maybe. I don't . . ." She rested her forehead on her knees.

"Leah?"

No answer.

"Leah!"

"What?" She jerked her head up, eyes momentarily wild.

"Are you okay?"

"Yeah, fine."

Matt started forward. "You don't look fine."

"Well, I am," Leah said. "Just fine." Her voice was brittle.

"Okay, sorry." He grabbed the snowshoes and trudged some distance away, unable to say more. He was trembling, he realized. Tired. Hungry. Scared. Injured. Overwhelmed. It all churned together like a toxic soup inside him; it backed up in his throat like a clogged drain, threatening to choke him. He hated feeling this way. Helpless. Useless. It was a quivering, blown-apart feeling, like he had shattered something priceless. And there was no way to fix it. No way to get it back.

The last time he felt this useless was when his father left. That last night he was in the house, the last night they'd all been together as a family. But Matt had no idea it would be the last night. Over the years this fact infuriated him, to know that he had been deceived so easily. That he had no clue at all. If he had, maybe he would have done something different. As it was, the evening had been insanely normal, and he followed the same bedtime routine he always had. Pajamas, wash face, brush teeth, floss. Even though he was almost twelve at the time, his father still read stories with him at night, and after a chapter in the current book they were reading, Matt opened to a random page in his new *Ultimate Quote Book*, placing his finger blindly on a sentence. He spoke the words slowly.

"What you are will show in what you do."

"Very nice." His father smiled, looking down at the page. "Who said that one?"

"Thomas Edison."

"Good, good." His father nodded. "That man was a great scientist. A genius." Then he tucked Matt in, kissed his forehead, and said, "Good night, Matty." He turned off the light and the glow stars on Matt's ceiling bloomed pale green in the dark.

But his father sat on the end of his bed for a long time, and after a few minutes Matt pretended to fall asleep, breathing heavily through his mouth. When his father finally got up, the bedsprings creaked a bit, but it was a different sound that got his attention. That should have been the clue, Matt knew now. He should have known. It was a weird noise, something he'd never heard before, something he'd never heard since. But he didn't have to have heard it before to know what it was. He'd never be able to forget that sound.

His father was crying.

The next morning, he was gone.

"I think there's something wrong with my feet." Matt propped his right foot over his left knee, then carefully tugged off the first layer. Then, as though he was opening a bag full of rotten garbage, he eased off the second sock.

His foot. Actually his toes. Specifically, his big toe. Stained as though dipped in ink; his second toe similar but not as dark. Both were swollen with shiny blisters, evil, pus-filled balloons he had a perverse desire to pop. Whatever Matt had been expecting to see, it wasn't that. It was almost too grotesque to be real—like a bad special effects makeup job, applied by a blind person.

"Matt . . . oh my God." Leah sucked in her breath, and for a second it looked like she might be sick. "Why didn't you say something?"

He sat there, unable to do anything but stare at his foot. His remaining toes were various shades of pink and red, white-tipped but normal size.

Leah knelt down and ripped off her gloves, covering the damage with her bare hands. She was obviously not the squeamish type; something about her gesture knotted Matt's throat shut.

"It hurts," he finally gurgled. "What do I do?"

"We're gonna get out of here. We'll get you to a doctor. . . ."

"Don't . . ." He shook his head, wondering how he would get out of this, how he'd be able to make it the rest of the way. He wished he hadn't looked. And now he couldn't unsee it. "You said you wanted to know about me? About my family? Did you know I'm finally going to have a sibling?" Matt didn't wait for her answer, he just kept speaking. "All my life I wanted a brother or sister. And now my idiot father just told me that his twenty-eight-year-old girlfriend is pregnant. That's why I'm here," he babbled. "I wasn't supposed to be here. My parents were supposed to get back together. They weren't supposed to get divorced. I even memorized the whole damn quote book he gave me, like it was some kind of test." He buried his face in his hands. "Every page. Every line."

"Why, Matt?" Leah's hands gripped around his rotten-looking foot like a vise. "Why did you do that?"

"I thought if I knew everything I could figure out the answer."

"The answer?"

"The answer to why he left." His voice cracked. "Why we weren't *good* enough for him. Why he wanted to start over with someone else." He looked up to keep the tears from spilling, hoping they would freeze instead.

Leah was quiet for a while. "There isn't an answer to that. People do things and they don't even know why."

"I thought I could fix it if I knew why."

Silence. Wind in the branches. The sun was gone now, the sky above them dull and solid, the color of cold, wet cement.

"And now I'm gonna die out here."

"No, Matt. You're not."

"Maybe the baby will be a girl. Maybe they'll tell her stories about me." Matt wiped his eyes. "Maybe they'll tell her about her brother. The one who died out in the mountains before she was born."

"Stop it!"

"It would be a good story. After all, they'd say he helped rescue his friends. . . ."

"Shut! Your! Mouth!"

A *whump* of snow hit the ground from a nearby tree. A bird launched into flight, startled by Leah's outburst. A great horned owl passed overhead, only to land in another towering evergreen. It peered down at them with wide gold eyes.

Leah sat back on her haunches, Matt's black toes and blisters forgotten as they watched the sky, the trees, each other. Her eyes were the only warm thing he saw, simmering brown with tears of her own. A long time passed before she spoke.

"I used to think it was my fault too. Being in foster

care." She examined her hands, as if contact with his feet might have been a bad idea, as if he had leprosy, not frostbite. "Even though I knew deep down it wasn't. I couldn't help it. The guilt was . . ." Her lips flattened to a microscopic line. "I think it was worse for Carter. He idolized our mom." After a moment she sighed, stood up, and shook her head, as if to shake the thought away. "How's the other one?"

It took him a second to understand she was referring to his other foot, and he slowly removed his sock, holding his breath. No darkness there. Not yet. He pinched the white tips, denting the skin with his fingernails, relieved to feel the sting, and watched the bloodflow rush back under the skin, returning them to pink.

"Okay," she said. "So far so good. We shouldn't have much farther to go." She held out a hand, and he wondered if *much farther* meant a mile or ten. "Can you walk?" By the tone in her voice it was clear to Matt that the pity party was over.

"Do I have a choice?"

"Well, technically you do." For a moment she looked as though she wanted to pat his arm, say it was going to be just fine, tell him not to worry. Matt knew that wasn't her style. It wasn't his either. "But there's only one good choice. And it's downhill from here."

Ten minutes later it was snowing again, but as they moved farther down the mountain it morphed into sleet.

"We're getting close." Leah leaned against a slim aspen for support, sagging into it with a tired hug. "Either a road or a stream. That's all we need."

She's exhausted, Matt thought. *She still might be hypothermic.* Or maybe it was coming back. Leah had removed her hat and unzipped her coat despite the increasing wind, acting as if she were overheated instead of freezing. Was that a sign of hypothermia? He couldn't remember. What Matt did remember was what happened the last time they found a stream. "I hope it's a road."

"I doubt anyone will be out driving around in this." Leah rested her cheek against the aspen's stippled bark.

"True." Sleet was worse than snow, Matt decided. It was rain's colder and meaner sister. "I'm sorry I said all that stuff back there."

"What stuff?" Leah's hair was wet down her back, darkening from copper to a shade of blood-soaked brown. The ends curled under into smooth, tight hooks. "You mean about your dad?"

"Yeah," Matt said. "Just everything I said. It's stupid. I'm stupid."

"Only really smart people say they're stupid," Leah said. "And what you said wasn't stupid at all."

"But compared to you . . ." He couldn't finish. Shame swelled his tongue like an allergic reaction.

"Compared to me?" Leah said, squinting. "You mean because I was in foster care?"

"Well, yeah."

"I guess." She shrugged. "I mean, I went into the system when I was three or so. Carter was four, almost five. Honestly, I didn't really know any different."

"Well, I'm sorry anyway. Did your parents pass away or something?" *Pass away?* What a lame expression.

"Or something," she said, as though she had rehearsed it many times. A scattering of freckles stretched across her cheeks with her forlorn smile. "We stayed with a foster family for a few years. A bit religious, but nice." She gave the tree another hug. "It wasn't all bad, not like some of the horror stories people hear. But then, when I was eight and Carter was nine, we left."

"Really? Why?"

"Because that's when our mom came back," she explained. "Clean and sober, or so she said."

He relaxed. "So it worked out all right, then?"

"No, Matt. It didn't work out at all." She sank down, eyes closed, legs splayed out, and for a moment Matt thought she had fainted. "Leah!" He grabbed on to her elbow, touched her cheek.

She opened her eyes with some effort, staring up at him. But it was a blank look, as though she didn't know who he was. "But this time she OD'd," she whispered. "She didn't wake up. Carter was the one who found her."

Matt wondered what that would do to someone, to find a dead person curled up in their bed or slumped in a chair. And not just a dead person. Your own mother. How long did Carter try to wake his mother until he figured it out. A minute? Five? What happens when you realize? What do you say? What do you do?

Overhead, the sky was a pure gray light. No clouds. No sun. He held her hands in his. It wouldn't hurt to sit and rest for a few minutes, at least until it stopped sleeting. Matt retrieved the tarp from his pack and unfolded it over them, making a small shield against the unrelenting wet. "How did you not go crazy?"

"The library."

"The library?"

Her laugh was weak. *Broken*, was the word Matt thought. "Before everything went down the shitter in Boise—that's where we had been living—Carter and I would go to the public library. Carter did a lot on the computers, but I mostly read. We'd pack a lunch and spend the whole day there."

"Wow."

"Well, it was a lot better than hanging out in our crappy apartment," she explained. "That's how I found George Eliot. Silas Marner was my favorite." She smiled wryly. "Can you guess why?"

"I think so." Matt nodded, recalling the plot. Old Silas Marner, the town recluse, was something of a miser. A money hoarder with no friends. One day he came home to find all his gold stolen, and a little girl left sleeping in its place. Silas raised her as his own daughter, and at the end the original thief is found drowned at the bottom of a pond with all the stolen gold. By this time the girl has grown up, and because of her Silas is now a respected member of the community, his lonely miser life redeemed by a little orphan girl's love.

"It's never too late to be who you might have been."

"Who said that?" Matt blinked; he didn't know that quote. It wasn't in the *Ultimate Quote Book*. He had the thing memorized. And he would have remembered that one.

"That's George Eliot," she said, sounding pleased. "But her real name was Mary Anne Evans."

"I didn't know that, either."

"My mother had the same name. Mary Evans."

"Your last name is Evans?"

"Yep. I'm Leah Anne Evans."

"I'm Matthew Joseph Ruban," Matt said. "Nice to finally meet you."

"The pleasure's all mine." She closed her eyes. Matt watched the thin capillaries on her eyelids, the small pulse of blood under the skin. The constellation of freckles across her nose. The tiny diamond stud in her nostril. She looked almost happy. "Too bad we had to meet like this."

"No kidding."

"I guess it could be worse."

"Well," Matt yawned, "when I get out of here I'm never leaving my house again." An image sprang forth of him lying on the couch with an entire pepperoni-and-jalapeño pizza. Paradise. The snowdrift felt like a blanket around them, heavy and snug. *It wouldn't be the worst idea to have a quick nap*, he thought.

"I can't wait to see the world."

"Really?"

"As soon as I turn eighteen," she said, keeping her eyes closed. "I'll be able to go. I already have my passport."

"I've never been out of the country," Matt said sleepily.

"I've never been anywhere," Leah said. "I'm saving up for my first ticket."

"Where?"

"Hawaii."

"Mmm." Hawaii sounded perfect to Matt. Warm sun, warm sand, warm water. Everything warm. By this point it felt physically impossible to keep his eyes open. Too much work. His eyelids fluttered weakly.

"Those islands," Leah murmured. "Green mountains, volcanoes, the water, the palm trees, the flowers. Black sand beaches. Tropical sunsets."

"Sssounds nice." Matt sighed. They shouldn't fall asleep, he thought briefly. No, not sleep. Just a little nap. Just until the weather let up. Because they had something they needed to do. They needed to keep moving, but a short rest would help. For the first time in days he felt comfortable. The pain in his feet seemed to have dulled. That was good. Definitely an improvement. He yawned again and dropped his chin to his chest. Leah slumped her head on his shoulder, and the sleet came down faster, a few minutes later changing back to snow. It enveloped them in a soft swirl of white.

Matt bolted up. Sheets of snow cascaded from his hat, his parka, sifting down over him. His breath came in short gasps. What was it? Something woke him. A bad dream? He was sweaty, disoriented, and the skin on his neck crawled. "Leah?" His voice was a thin whisper. No answer. He pushed his shoulder against hers; her breath was warm against his cheek. Had she made that noise? No, she slept on, dead to the world. *Dead to the world.* He shouldn't think those words. Not now.

Matt's heart raced. His throat was raw and hot, as though he'd sprinted a mile. Why? He'd just been sitting here sleeping. Had it been a bad dream? How long had they been here unconscious? He stared out into the hazy white, his eyes trying to land on something solid, something that wasn't snowflakes.

Prickles crawled up his scalp, but it was not from the cold. A creepy tingle behind his ears, as though he were being watched, and without even comprehending it, his muscles tightened, starting at his jaw and moving down. Chest, arms, stomach, thighs, calves. His hands curled into fists. He stared again into the white, willing something to appear and confirm his fears.

Black and gold. Gold against so much white. Blinking, he looked again through the thickening curtain of snow and held his breath. A hallucination? No. It was there. He couldn't dream something like this. "Leah, wake up."

"Mmmm."

"Leah," he whispered against her cheek, never once taking his eyes from the distant shape. "Are there mountain lions here?"

Leah jerked away as if he'd just pinched her. "Where?"

"Look straight ahead. Through that aspen row. A hundred yards out."

"I don't see it. I see some boulders."

"Look up," he whispered. "Above that spot."

It moved then, as if it heard and understood what he had said. Tawny fur, black tail tip, flecked with snow, the unmistakable liquid feline gait. Leah sucked in her breath. "Let's go."

"Do you think it will follow us?"

"Maybe," she said. "Maybe it doesn't see us. Or maybe it's just curious."

"Not hunting us?"

She shifted uncomfortably, her breath coming fast. "I've heard of them going after dogs."

"Not people?"

"Maybe a person by themselves," she replied, never taking her eyes off the cat. They watched as it slunk between the trees, moving higher up the slope, blending in with the rocks. "I think they're normally afraid of people."

He needed something sturdy, something for defense, and settled on a tree limb the size and length of a club.

When he picked it up he was surprised at its lightness. The wood must have rotted; he feared one hit would shatter it. Still, it was better than nothing.

He stood motionless in the swirling snowfall, the dead branch balanced lightly over his shoulder like a gnarled baseball bat. He stared at the trees for movement. Past dusty green spruces and giant blue-needled firs, between slim aspens and their black spiderlike branch tips swollen and ready to bud. Though the forest was silent, he knew it was there. And he knew it was watching. But they couldn't run.

Not anymore.

So Matt waited. Ignoring the throb pulsing through his ruined feet, he wished for the hundredth time that he was somewhere else—anywhere else. Despite all the things that had happened in the past three days, or maybe because of them, Matt refused to accept that he would die here. Not now. Not like this. Not after everything they'd gone through. Then again, he figured there must be a limit to luck—it had to run out eventually. This was just as good a time as any. Just as good a place. Out here, death came easy.

But he wasn't going to die without a fight.

The snow fell faster; thick, feathery flakes obliterated the landscape around him into a downy blur. The trees disappeared; the mountains beyond them vanished. No birdcalls, no wind, no sound at all except his own breath.

He exhaled small puffs of steam and waited.

And waited . . .

"Matt?"

He blinked. *Where is it? Where am I? How long have I been standing here?* The snow seemed to be messing with his vision. He looked left, right, up and down. He held his breath and counted to ten. But no, it had vanished. Like it had never been there at all. He tightened his grip on the branch.

"We should go," Leah said, after what felt like an hour. "If we stay together we should be fine."

"Should be fine?" Matt noticed she had found her own stick, shorter and stubbier than his.

They trudged slowly through the uneven drifts. Even if they had the energy to run it would have been impossible. Still, the urge was there, and Matt could not resist checking behind him every few seconds. The snow tapered to sparse flurries after a few minutes, and they found a trail between the trees. He glanced down for any tracks, but the snow melted under their feet as they stumbled along. Soon enough, though, he saw what he'd been looking for, distinct and wide as his hand. "Is that what I think it is?"

"Uh-huh." Leah swallowed noisily.

A few feet ahead there were more, spread out and curving in front of them in an arc. "Where did it go?"

Leah spied another track, turning back toward the rise. "Looks like it circled back."

A new crop of goose bumps rose on his neck. It was

behind them, as he had feared, and although he knew it was just an animal, incapable of deceit or evil intentions, he was suddenly horrified they were being hunted.

Run! he thought. *No. Wait. Don't run! You're never supposed to run.*

But Matt wasn't sure. He used his stick to walk faster, because his feet no longer were cooperating, and it took most of his effort not to trip. His left foot tingled, the way the right one once had been, a warning sign. Another step forward over a rock and he stumbled, slipping down the snow-slicked path.

"Matt!" Leah tugged at his sleeve. "Slow down! It's getting too steep."

The slope was now a forty-five-degree angle at best, sparsely treed. A lot more rock and a lot less snow. And what was there was slick and hard. He slid to a halt, ready to tell her he couldn't help it, that they needed to run, when he heard a sound so sharp and piercing it turned his guts to water. It was like someone had pulled a plug and everything inside his body had just drained out.

A scream. Only something inhuman could have produced it. Every single hair on his body stood to attention. Vaulting forward, he slipped and grabbed a tree branch and spun around backward. "Leah! Hurry!" Out of the corner of his eye he saw it, a galloping blur, covering the distance between the trees in impossibly long jumps. It was coming. It was already here.

But Leah wasn't hurrying. She just stood there, and as

the cat jumped to her, she raised the club over her head and howled. The wood made a sickening thud on impact, but it had merely hit the animal's rib cage, not its head. It didn't stop, but grabbed her around the legs as she turned, tackling her faster than any NFL linebacker. She landed face down as Matt scrambled back up the slope, waving his own stick like a samurai warrior, and screamed. He wasn't scared anymore. He wasn't anything. He had become what Shakespeare had written. Full of sound and fury, signifying nothing. He could only hope that he wasn't being an idiot as well.

He swung the club with everything he had, the cat's head the ninety-five-mile-an-hour fastball he needed to annihilate.

Upon contact, the stick did break, splintering into over a dozen pieces. An explosion of wood. The cat screamed in pain, momentarily forgetting Leah, and it sprang back, spitting venomously. Even crouched down on its haunches with its ears flattened, it was huge. It snarled at Matt with pure hatred, sinking lower to the ground, its pupils narrowing to furious black slits.

"C'mon!" Matt screamed, blind drunk with rage. It was something he'd wanted; he'd been waiting for it. After all these years he'd been itching for this fight, and there was a deeply satisfying fury building inside him, rising to the surface. He should be afraid. But there was no more room. Blood roared in his ears. There would be no holding back, no pulling punches. He opened his arms wide. It was all there inside him—coiled, hissing, alive. He was as wild as the animal in front of him. *Let it come,* he thought. *I'm ready.* "Come and get me, you son of a bitch!"

The cat leaped toward him as if shot from a cannon, all too eager to obey.

When the mountain lion hit Matt in the chest, flinging him backward without a sound, they slammed to the ground in a ferocious embrace and somersaulted backward. Because of the steep slope, the momentum kept them both going, Matt drawing up his knees in an attempt to push the cat off. But it was like trying to rid himself of a straitjacket. He felt his back and neck crack as they tumbled; he smelled the animal's breath, rank and steamy, against his face. But he didn't see. He kept his eyes squeezed shut, forearms wedged in front to protect his stomach, chest, and head. A sharp burst of light on his shoulder. The cat's claws or teeth, something had clamped down, pierced the nylon parka. He screamed. Or was it the cat? They were locked together so tightly he no longer knew what the rest of his body was doing. Still they kept falling, crashing down between the trees.

"Matt! Grab on to something!" But Leah's voice was thin, drifting away in the distance.

"I'm trying!" But there was nothing to grab. And that seemed to be the least of his worries. With his right arm he brought his elbow up into a V, turned his free shoulder in, and wedged a space between his chest and the cat's stomach. He jabbed hard, swinging his fist out as if in a knife stab, and struck its soft belly. The cat growled, slightly stunned, releasing its teeth from his shoulder. Matt twisted frantically, spinning back, and crashed through a scraggly bush, sharp branches puncturing his palms through his gloves. The cat rolled with him, hissing and spitting and yowling, but now Matt had one arm in a chokehold around the cat's neck. With his free hand he grabbed the branch, but the shoots were thin and flexible as whips. It was like trying to grab wet noodles. He had no hold. Still struggling, he let go and fell backward, slamming the cat to the ground and knocking the back of his head in the process, which miraculously landed on dirt and not a rock. He flipped to his stomach, using the same technique he tried last time, and because there was no ice he did slow down.

"Urrff!" He landed feetfirst in an awkward squat over the cat, cursing as shock waves radiated up his spine. Unfortunately, he didn't stop; the terrain was too steep, and they half ran, half bounced down the hillside another few feet before tumbling off a narrow ledge. Even while falling, the cat maintained its predatory instinct, ignoring the fear of gravity. Seconds later, the sharp crack of water against Matt's face almost knocked him out cold.

The river! His limbs banged against hidden rocks; icy water swelled over his head, but he felt his boots touch bottom, scraping along as he was carried like a leaf. The current was too fast, and he was too weak and exhausted. The cat had splashed in with him, but now was nowhere to be seen.

I can't get stuck, he thought. *I can't get trapped.* He was already too far downstream for Leah to catch him. He didn't hear her anymore. Where was she? Where was the cat? Immediately, he pulled his knees in to his chest, trying to float over the boulders, trying to make himself as small as possible, when he finally saw something he'd been hoping all along to find.

A bridge.

A bridge meant a trail, and a trail meant a way back to civilization. Civilization meant people, help, and food. He dog-paddled to the right side, looking for anyone who could be coming down the trail, wondering if he could grab on. It was a small, crude-looking stone arch, rising a few feet above the swollen rapids.

"Matt!" Leah stood on the bridge, leaning precariously over the side, but it was useless. She was screaming something. A word he couldn't make out. The current splashed over his head. He couldn't stop. If he grabbed for her hands he would only pull her in. All he could do now was try not to drown.

As he was swept underneath the bridge, he reached his hand up, missing hers by a foot. He swirled past like a leaf. On the other side rocks jutted up, breaking the surface, turning the water to froth. Now everything hit against him, slamming with solid, unyielding punches.

Leah screamed as Matt was swept around the bend, and when the river spun him again, he finally understood the word she'd been yelling.

Waterfall.

This time there was no rope. There was no help, no rescue. It was only him, only the river, only gravity. And the edge came fast, rushing up to him the way Dennis Greene's fists once came rushing up to his face. But this time he didn't fight back. There was only one thing to do: take a deep breath.

He flew over the edge, for a few moments completely weightless, completely free. The river below him was a pearly thread, shimmering in blue-green opalescence as the sun broke through the clouds. And as it lit up the sky, gilding the trees and rocks and snow, only one thought came to him, unexpected and true.

It is so beautiful.

"Is he dead?"

"I don't think so."

"Well, he looks dead."

"Nah."

"So poke him then, Rosie."

"Why don't you, Sasha?"

"I don't touch dead bodies. Not sanitary. And it's not standard operating procedure."

"Uhhhh," Matt moaned and rolled over, and immediately decided that was a mistake. Rocks pressed painfully into his back and shoulders. He spat a mouthful of water. "Owwwww!"

"See? I told you he wasn't dead."

"Leah?" he croaked.

"And he's talking so I think he's fine. He looks human."

"Right now I'm thinking he looks more like a zombie."

"Zombies aren't real, Rosie."

"That's what they want you to think, Sasha."

Matt cracked his eyes open. Above him were two girls, maybe ten years old—one with a blond ponytail and the other with long dark braids. Underneath their navy-blue fleece jackets, they wore army-green shirts and pants, with gold sashes draped diagonally across their shirts, decorated with complicated badges, insignia, and metal pins. "Where am I?"

"Earth," said the dark braid girl.

"Good lord, Sasha," interrupted the blonde. "He's not an alien."

"Just covering my bases, Rosie. Don't assume. Remember the manual?"

Their conversation was confusing to Matt; they didn't sound like young girls. Instead, they spoke like military personnel—very small military personnel. He coughed; spasms racked his chest. "Where's Leah?"

"Who?"

"We were hiking." He struggled to sit up, and the girls moved back a few steps when he did, keeping their distance. "A mountain lion attacked . . . fell in the river . . .

went over the waterfall. . . ." He stopped, wondering how crazy he must sound, how he must look. He was soaking wet, but he had no idea how he swam to shore, or even if he did swim. "Can you get me an ambulance, please?" he asked, stupid with cold. "I think I need to go to a hospital."

"No kidding, mister." The blond one called Rosie snorted. "It's already on the way."

"I need to find Leah."

"I think he means the red-haired girl," Sasha whispered.

"You've seen her?" He struggled to his feet, but his knees were jelly. His legs wouldn't obey. He put his weight on his left side, but a lightning bolt of pain in his ankle made him yelp. He fell back down in a shaking heap. "I think my ankle is broken."

"Yeah, mister." Rosie looked him over, unimpressed, almost disappointed. Maybe she had been hoping he was a zombie, if only to prove her companion wrong. "You look like crap on a cracker, as my dad would say."

"That girl Leah found our unit," Sasha told him as Rosie texted something on what looked like a cell phone. Or maybe it was a walkie-talkie. "Said you went over the falls. They relayed the approximate coordinates. We figured you'd end up here if you survived."

If he survived. "You're just kids," he sputtered, trying not to wince as he felt along his ankle. The skin was bloated, puffy with damage. He pulled his fingers away. "What are you even doing out here?"

"Rescue badges!" they chirped back.

"We volunteered for ground search today," Rosie added. "When the call came through the dispatch, my dad told me."

Matt stared at her, confused.

"Her dad's the sheriff in this county," Sasha said.

"Are you Girl Scouts or something?"

"Heck no!" Rosie gagged. "We're the WGW."

"The what?"

"Wilderness Girl Warriors," Sasha explained.

Matt saw an entire arsenal of equipment attached to their utility belts. A rope. A bungee cord. A flashlight. A compass. A Swiss army knife. A carabiner clip. A whistle. Bear repellant spray. It was quite possible they were also outfitted with Tasers. Maybe grenades.

"Here." Sasha tossed him a small plastic bag filled with peanuts, dried fruit, and chocolate chips. "Have some gorp. You look like you need it."

Matt did need it; he inhaled it. And after he was done he turned the bag inside out and licked it, refusing to miss a grain of salt or a smear of chocolate.

"Oink, oink." Rosie glanced at her phone. "All right. Base command has our location. Setting up for a rendez-vous and extraction. The cavalry is on the way."

Sasha handed Matt her canteen. "You're lucky we found you when we did, mister. It's gonna be dark soon."

"Thank you," he said as he accepted it. "By the way,

my name is Matt." After he finished drinking he handed it back. "And you're right. I *am* lucky."

The setting sun stretched their shadows out as they waited at the river's edge, enlightening him with adventurous tales of the Wilderness Girl Warriors. Despite his frostbitten toes, his broken ankle, and his shivering (most likely hypothermic) battered body, he had never felt more satisfied than he did right now, listening to them explaining how to set a proper tripwire, how to shoot a moving target, the right colors of green and brown face paint for camouflage. The white noise of the waterfall was like a hum in his blood, and he sat quietly and listened patiently, knowing he'd finally been rescued, saved by a pair of ten-year-old commandos.

It had been a good day.

DAY 7

MATT

Location: University of Colorado Hospital, Aurora, Colorado

Matt knew he'd been out for a few days because when he woke up the first thing his eyes landed on was his mother, sitting in the little side chair next to his hospital bed. She was reading a book, a clue she'd been there a while, and it was also a clue she was relaxed, which must have meant the doctors had already reassured her he would be fine.

Right now, if he was honest, he felt better than fine. The lumpy hospital mattress underneath him a cloud of soft fluff. Smooth sheets against his skin, the solid weight of blankets pulled up to his chin, leaving him pleasantly cocooned. Even his eyes had a weight, and when he tried to wipe them, his mother looked up from her book. "Oh honey!" Her face alternated first with surprise, then worry, before she finally smiled and settled on relief. "You're awake!"

"Mom?" It was hard to make his mouth work; his tongue felt bloated to twice its size. Or maybe it was the drugs. They must have given him something. After all, he was in a hospital—druggie heaven.

"I'm here, honey." She squeezed his hand in hers, but it felt far away, a phantom itch on his skin. "Your dad's here too. He just went to get some coffee."

Coffee. It sounded amazing. "Me too," he babbled. "I want some too."

"Okay honey." She smiled. "The surgeon will be coming by soon to explain a few things. He wanted to talk to you when you woke up."

"Surgeon? Why?"

She kept patting his hand, her face an undecipherable mask. She leaned over and smoothed his hair back from his forehead, then kissed it, like she used to do when he was little.

"Matthew!" His father appeared at the end of his bed, holding two Styrofoam cups of coffee. He was rumpled looking, like he'd slept in his clothes. Or hadn't slept at all. "Good morning. Or should I say good afternoon." He set the cups down on the table. "How do you feel, son?"

"Hungry," he confessed. "Really hungry. Do they have pancakes here?"

"I think that can be arranged." His dad smiled, eyes wet and shining. He was here. Matt realized he hadn't seen him in over a month. Or heard his voice.

His mom released his hand, placed his arm across his chest as though she were arranging him into a proper position. "I'll go and let the nurses know you're awake."

She kissed him once more, gave a silent nod to Matt's dad, and slipped out the door. He wondered what they had talked about while he was sleeping, but he already knew he would never ask.

"Matt." His father sat down heavily in the chair, bent his head forward so he was staring at his coffee. "I wanted . . ."

"I'm sorry, Dad."

"Sorry?" He looked up. "What on Earth do you have to be sorry for?"

"For what I said on the phone." Matt took a breath. "I shouldn't have said it."

"Well, what you said was true." His father smiled back at his cup. "I think I am an idiot."

"I still shouldn't have said it."

"I shouldn't have canceled our trip. Shannon had some problems and . . ."

"Is she okay?" Matt's voice was rough with worry.

His father glanced at him, surprised at his sudden concern. "Oh yes. Yes, she's fine. But she didn't want to be alone, just in case . . ." He trailed off, looking up at a painting on the wall. A picture of mountains, a view of a snow-covered range sometime near sunrise.

"I understand." Matt did understand, in a way he hadn't before, and he examined the painting as well, wondering if they both saw the same image. Doubtful. Matt knew he would never look at mountains the same way again.

His father put his hand on Matt's shoulder, squeezed it, but Matt winced. "Ow!"

"What is it?" He snatched his hand back as if burned.

Matt rolled his shoulder. A thick square of gauze was taped on the top, poking out through the hospital gown. "That's where the mountain lion bit me." He turned his head, as if to look at it, wondering how many stitches it took. "At least, that's what I think it is. Honestly, when these drugs wear off I think everything's gonna hurt."

"Mountain lion?" His father was stunned. He sank back into the chair like a deflated balloon. "Jesus Christ, Matt."

"Yeah."

There was not much else to say after a confession like that. "You look different," his father offered finally.

"Well, I definitely lost a few pounds."

"It's not that," his father said. "I don't know, really. I guess you look older."

"I feel older."

"You're not a kid anymore, that's for sure." His father scratched at his chin. "When did that happen?"

Matt gave the picture one last look, finally recognizing it—the view was the same outside the window. "It happened a few days ago."

"Knock, knock."

Matt turned his head. Next to his mother, a man in green scrubs stood in the doorway. Green hat. Green shirt. Green pants. This must be the surgeon. "I heard the patient is awake." He walked into the room and stood at the end of the hospital bed, giving Matt a satisfied smile.

"Yes, doctor," his dad immediately replied, gratitude (and something like awe) in his voice.

But if he's a surgeon he must have done some sort of operation, Matt thought. *On me. But what . . .*

His feet. His toes. His legs.

"No!" Matt leaned forward, flinging off the blankets. He couldn't feel anything, see anything.

"Honey! It's okay!" His mom pressed a solid hand to his chest, pushing him back down to his pillow. "Calm down."

"My feet!" he blared, but it came out wrong. It sounded like *mwah fwee*.

"You're fine." His mom understood. "Your feet are just fine." She helped prop him up; his dad adjusted the mechanical bed. His right leg, he now saw, was bandaged from the shin down, wrapped up so it resembled an enormous Q-tip. His left leg was encased in a bootlike cast, all the way up to his knee.

The surgeon stood at the end of the bed. Matt thought he looked young—much too young to be in charge of cutting people open. "I hear you have a pretty amazing story to tell."

"What did you do to me?"

"Well, you get right to the point, don't you?" He grinned and bobbed his head good-naturedly. "It's not so bad. Just the big toe. *That* definitely had to go. Completely necrotic. And part of the second metatarsal."

"What?" Matt gasped. "You *cut off* my toes?"

"Right ankle was shattered, too. I put in three screws," he continued, as though he were commenting on the weather. "All things considered, it looks good. You're one tough nut, kid."

Shattered ankle. That must have happened in his plunge over the falls. Leah must have told the doctors everything else.

Leah! "I wasn't alone," he said, swallowing down something sour. "Where is she?"

"Where is who, honey?" his mom asked.

"Leah. She's the one who saved my life. More than once."

The surgeon looked down at his clipboard with a frown. "Yes, I remember her. She was adamant that she was fine. We treated her for mild hypothermia. Kept her overnight for observation, but she refused to be admitted." He looked up. "She left with her brother two days ago."

"You found them?" He gripped the edge of the sheets. "Where are they? Where's Tony?"

"Tony's fine. They're all fine, honey," his mom said.

He knew that wasn't true. "Sid was hurt bad, Mom."

"Well, he's going to recover," the doctor replied. "Thanks to you. That was real smart thinking, telling the nine-one-one operator the coordinates. The helicopter crew spotted the slide and were able to locate them quickly. If they hadn't, your friend wouldn't have lasted much longer."

"Sid's okay?"

"Punctured lung," his dad told him. "And a head injury. He's still here in the hospital, recovering like you. The Jains flew in with us on the same flight last night." He touched Matt on the head, something he hadn't done in years. "You saved them, son. I'm so proud of you."

Matt lay there, considering his words. "Dylan?" He felt a twinge of nausea at his name. "Did they find him too?"

His mother gave his father a look, as if they had already previously agreed on how much to tell him. "There's a recovery team out there right now, looking for Dylan's body. They have dogs. . . . And the girl, Julie . . ."

"What?" Matt looked up in surprise at her name. "What about Julie?"

"Well, they're still trying to figure that part out. I guess she skied off somewhere and they have some volunteers still looking." She patted his hand. "That boy Carter stopped by when you were in surgery. Such a nice young man. Said he and his sister were going back out to help look. That must be that Leah girl?"

"I can't believe she just left." Matt watched the ceiling. He counted the tiles running over it and got to fifteen before he found he could speak again. "I didn't get to say good-bye."

The surgeon cleared his throat, looked at his watch,

impatient to leave. "So, I just wanted to tell you the situation." He tapped his finger on Matt's cast.

"How long?" Matt was also eager to have the surgeon leave.

"Eight weeks," he replied. "You're young and strong. You'll want to make an appointment with an orthopedist when you return to Des Moines."

"How long till I can play basketball?"

"Well, ahh . . . you'll probably want to discuss that with your own doctor," he answered, rubbing his chin. "No hurry to rush it. Make sure to concentrate on getting your balance back to normal."

"So no basketball? No tennis? No anything?"

"Uh . . . ahh." He kept massaging his chin, as if trying to think of a more agreeable way to say no. "Have you ever considered golf? It's a great sport." He bobbed his head once more and gave them a weird wave as he backed out of the room, something between a bow and a salute. "And you can even ride around in a cart."

4 MONTHS LATER

MATT

Location: Home, West Des Moines, Iowa

"All ready, honey?"

"Yeah Mom."

"You sure you've got everything? Enough underwear and socks?"

"I'm good for at least two weeks." Matt stifled a laugh. "I know how to do laundry, remember?"

"I know." His mom blinked. She was smiling, but her eyes were too bright, too red and puffy around the edges. He knew she'd been crying. "What about snacks?"

"Got it," he replied. "And you can always send me care packages if you want." He knew she would; he knew she'd want to. "The cookies I like. You remember what kind?"

"Oatmeal chocolate chip." His mom nodded and bit her lip, chewing on it absently. Her hands fluttered as she moved about the kitchen, opening drawers and cabinets, then shutting them, wiping the dishrag over the same spot on the counter, as if waiting for a mess to appear.

"He'll be just fine, Rebecca," his grandfather said,

looking up from the table as he went through yesterday's mail. His mother's parents had flown in from their
retirement home in Arizona the week after he returned
to Iowa, and even though he'd been home for more than
four months, they were still here. Matt's mother still got
worried when he was out of her sight, but his grandfather
was more old school, and he liked to remind Matt that
when he was Matt's age he was getting shot at in a rice
paddy in Vietnam. The very first thing Grandpa Molinari
said when he arrived was a question, actually a demand.
"Let me see that foot of yours, kid." And when Matt
removed his sock, Grandpa whistled. "Holy sonsabitches!"
To which his grandmother hollered, "Leave the boy alone,
Peter! And stop your goddamn swearing!"

Matt wasn't sure what he meant, but Grandpa seemed
weirdly impressed with his injury because he clapped him
on the back and offered to take him down to the local
bar for a whiskey. Unfortunately, his mom said no. For his
first two weeks back, his mom hovered around him like
he was a toddler learning to walk, even going so far as
to sit in his room at night when he slept. He knew this
because he woke up once and saw her sitting in his desk
chair, head slumped on the table.

"Matt will be just fine," Grandpa Molinari repeated
adamantly. "Just fine. After all, he takes after me." He gave
Matt a conspiratorial wink.

"I know he'll be fine, Dad." His mother sighed. "But
it's a big change. And it's a big city."

"Minneapolis isn't so big," Matt argued. He was wearing his new University of Minnesota T-shirt—it came last night in the mail. He liked the maroon and gold combination better than he thought he would.

"Well, it's bigger than Des Moines."

"It'll be fine, Mom. It'll be good."

"I know," his mom said, shaking her head. "Oh, did you call Tony?"

"Yeah, the Jains left yesterday for Illinois."

"You two need to keep in touch." Her eyes grew even brighter at the mention of Tony's name. "Make sure you visit each other. I'm sure you're going to make a bunch of new friends, but . . ."

"We will." Matt nodded. "We definitely will." Matt and Tony had passed the summer in a quiet routine. Matt spent Monday and Wednesday mornings doing rehabilitation exercises at the clinic, mainly practicing keeping his balance while reaching and grabbing things, going up and down stairs, and other basic things he never realized required his toes. On Tuesdays, Thursdays, and Fridays he worked at the public library, learning to reshelve books according to the Library of Congress and Dewey decimal systems. And because Tony was working full-time at Kroger's, stocking shelves with cereal, pickles, jars of marinara, and baby wipes, it was always the evenings when they'd finally meet in Tony's driveway to shoot hoops. Sometimes Sid would be there, sitting in one of the Adirondack chairs in the front yard, and once in a while he'd join them, but would get winded after a few free throws. He was still recovering—unlike Matt, his injuries were hidden yet severe. It would take a long time for Sid to heal, and the doctors warned he would never be the way he was. Then again, neither would Matt and Tony.

They would shoot baskets until the sun sank behind the trees and the sky turned an incandescent shade of violet. Eventually the background would dissolve, the pole disappearing into the dim, leaving only a pale backboard to aim at. They'd play horse, round the world, twenty-one basketball, and time trial. But never one-on-one.

Once, after Tony had sunk five three-pointers in a row, he said, "I thought I saw her after." He held the ball against his chest like a shield.

"Saw who?"

"Julie."

Matt's heart skipped. They had learned that Julie's body had been recovered two weeks after they left Colorado. She had been found by a group of backpackers, near the base of a high cliff in a remote section of the forest. "What do you mean, *after?*"

Tony took another shot and the ball smacked the backboard, bouncing off onto the lawn. "After the helicopter picked us up. After we were flying back to Denver. I thought I saw her."

Matt didn't say anything for a while. He retrieved the ball from the grass. "What happened then?" He tossed the ball back to Tony.

"Nothing. Nothing happened." In the dark it was impossible to make out Tony's face, and Matt guessed he wanted it that way.

"Well," Matt said slowly, "maybe you didn't see her. Nobody else did?"

"No."

"Then maybe you didn't."

"Maybe." Tony didn't sound convinced.

Matt had the sensation his best friend wanted something from him that he wasn't qualified to provide. A pardon, absolution for his guilt, or possibly just a big fat lie. "Don't beat yourself up about it," he said finally. "You didn't do anything wrong." *That isn't a lie,* Matt thought.

This Tony seemed to accept. He dribbled the ball a few times, swallowed hard, and took another shot in the dark. And the net swooshed.

"What about your dad?" Matt's mother asked, snapping Matt out of his memories of late-night basketball games. "Did you get a chance to say good-bye?"

"We said good-bye last night," he replied, and by the sound of his voice she didn't ask any more. Her eyes remained focused on the counter, looking for stray crumbs to wipe away. "It's fine. It's good. He said that when things settle down, they all want to come up for a weekend. See the campus."

And that *all* included *her.* She was small, red-faced, and swaddled in white, a blue-and-pink-striped knit hat hiding dark hair when Matt first saw her in the maternity ward. Upon first glance Matt thought she looked rather squashed and wrinkly, more like an old elf than a baby. As he sat in the chair with her, snug in his arms, he wondered with a growing lump in his throat how something that delicate could survive in this world. "Hey, little baby," he said, and her eyes opened. First right, then left, and she peered up with twin pools of shining black, so deep and serene that he felt dizzy looking in them. Then the baby yawned and shut her eyes.

"Seven pounds, eight ounces," his father crowed. "Twenty inches long. A ten on the Apgar."

Matt had no idea what he was talking about, so he looked at Shannon, who was propped up in the bed. "Everything's perfect," she explained. "She's perfect." Shannon appeared exhausted, but not nearly as rough and worn out as his father. Her face was puffy, and her hair was limp and tangled, but Matt thought she looked beautiful. She *looked* like a mother.

"I still can't believe it," his father whispered as he took her from Matt's arms, handing her back to Shannon. "A girl. I was so sure it would be a boy." He shook his head in wonder. "I have no idea about girls."

"Me either," Matt said.

Shannon laughed. "You'll learn."

"So what's my sister's name?" Matt asked, trying the word out loud for the first time. *Sister.* He had a little sister.

"We can't decide," Shannon said. "We had agreed on the boys' names, but . . ."

"I still like Estelle," his dad offered. Matt wrinkled his nose. Estelle was his other grandmother's name. His mom's nickname for her was Battleaxe, among other things.

"No way." Shannon rolled her eyes, stared up at the ceiling. "It's not 1930, okay?"

"Well, I still like it." His dad shrugged. "Plus, you could nickname her Stella."

"I don't like nicknames," Shannon said. "Just one name. Simple and sweet."

"You haven't liked any of the names I've picked."

"It has to fit her." Shannon was unmoved. "It has to be right."

Matt watched the baby purse and relax her lips, as if she agreed with her mother's assessment. *A name that's simple and sweet.* Matt could think of one, even if the person who it belonged to was the opposite. He looked at his sister. It had to fit her. It had to be right.

"I know," Matt said suddenly, beaming into their expectant faces. "I know exactly what her name should be."

"Hmm." Grandpa Molinari picked up a small flyer from the stack of bills and ad inserts. "Strange." He directed his words to Matt, giving his feet a quick once-over. Matt wore his slip-on sport sandals, and though the surgeon did an excellent amputation job and everything healed nicely, with two toes missing his foot looked more like a flipper or some weird alien mutant appendage. He wondered if he'd ever get used to it. Probably not. But maybe he wasn't supposed to. "Very peculiar."

Matt thought he was still talking about his foot.

"What is very peculiar?" His mother kept scrubbing the same inch of countertop with the rag, like she was trying to bore a hole into it.

"Oh," his grandpa said. "Nothing. Just this." He held up the card, which Matt saw was a postcard. "It doesn't have a name on it." He flicked it onto the counter.

"Maybe it's the neighbor's and we got it by mistake." His mom turned it over, examining the writing. "Well, it has our address on it. That's peculiar."

A waterfall, all tropical greens and blues, and the picture started a twitch in Matt's throat. The temperature in the room seemed to double. It was hard to focus, and when he spoke his voice sounded far away, like he was calling out from the bottom of a canyon. "Where's it from?"

"Postmark from Hawaii," she said. "Maui."

"Well." His grandpa grinned. "That sounds nice. Who do we know in Hawaii?"

"Can I see it?" Matt held his hand out calmly when his mother passed it over, but the card trembled in his fingers. A small caption was written below the photograph. *The seven sacred pools of Ohe'o.* When he turned it over he didn't recognize the handwriting—he didn't have to.

There was only one sentence:

IT'S NEVER TOO LATE TO BE WHO YOU MIGHT HAVE BEEN.

"What is it, Matt?" His mom stared at him with such confusion that it took him a few moments to understand he was smiling. Smiling so wide his cheeks could split.

"It's not a mistake." His voice was thick, swelling inside him. "It came to the right house." Seven sacred pools. *Hawaii. Coconut palms, black sand beaches, turquoise water, and rainbow sunsets. Paradise.*

Leah.

"Oh," she said. "Okay, so who's it for?"

When he looked up again his eyes mirrored hers, shiny as newly minted coins. He pressed the postcard to his chest, his heart thumping in time with the words. "It's for me."

ACKNOWLEDGMENTS

When I was seventeen I climbed a mountain. And if I'd known how hard it would be, I most likely wouldn't have done it. Ignorance can sometimes be bliss. Other times it hurts. A lot. Still, I'm glad I went because I learned things on that mountain that I carry with me today, although, like most life-changing experiences, you don't usually realize it as it's happening. Instead, you're probably swearing and sweating and wondering why you're so stupid.

Writing a book is in many ways like climbing a mountain—swearing, sweating, and being stupid. Thinking you'll never make it. Wondering why you even tried. But then you get to the top and you finally understand. Of course, then you have to go back down. So it's a good idea not to try it alone.

Special thanks to Hannah Bowman for all her support, and deep gratitude to my editor, Nicole Ellul, at Simon Pulse for her encouragement, dedication, and insight. A special shout-out to Beth Adelman for her amazing copyediting work and to everyone at Simon Pulse who put so much time and energy into this story.

I'd like to thank my brother, James Dahlstrom, who not only told me his own backcountry skiing stories, but put me in touch with a former coworker at Grand Teton National Park—park ranger extraordinaire Ryan Schuster. Ryan, thank you so much for taking time out of your busy schedule (of literally saving people's lives) and talking to me about the finer points of mountain and helicopter rescue. If I am ever so unfortunate to find myself in a situation like that, I'm reassured that there are people like you out there, ready and waiting. I'd like to let the reader know that any mistakes about what I've described are entirely my own.

Thank you to Becca, Peter, Will, and Sasha for letting me steal your names!

Much thanks to my husband, Matt, whom I named the main character after. Yeah, you're welcome! After all the years we spent together and all the traveling we've done, I know that even if you aren't a Navy Seal, you're still pretty good under pressure. If I have to end up lost in the wilderness, I guess I'd want to be lost with you.

Finally, and most of all, thank you to my daughter Sena. Soon you will be seven, and in ten years maybe you'll want to climb your own mountain. Which means I better start getting ready.

On one last note, the National Park Service is celebrating their one-hundredth anniversary this year.

This amazing American creation is probably one of our country's greatest achievements, and if you have the chance, get out there and see our national parks.

Go get lost and found in the wild.

Just remember to bring a friend.

ALL EMMA WANTED WAS TO ESCAPE INTO THE MASSIVE WILDERNESS OF THE RUGGED BOUNDARY WATERS.

BUT MOTHER NATURE HAD OTHER PLANS. . . .

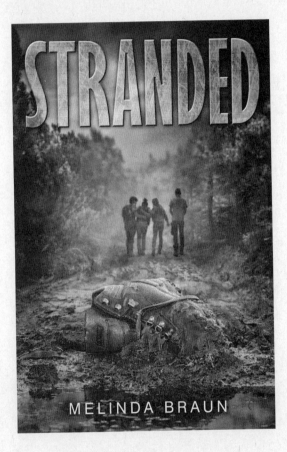

READ ON FOR A SNEAK PEEK AT
MELINDA BRAUN'S SURVIVAL DRAMA *STRANDED*.

One Year Ago

I inhaled and choked. No air. Just cold, dirty water, thick with grit, rushing into my mouth.

Instantly my throat contracted, squeezing shut as my lungs refused the liquid. Gagging, I spit back.

Help me!

Panic shot my hands out, snapping my eyes open. Green fog stared back, everything a watery blur. My arms jerked spastically; my legs followed.

No! I heaved forward, but the strap across my chest wrenched me back. My fingers fluttered automatically, an instinctual muscle memory, until they found the release button.

My chest burned, despite the cold, and my hands scrambled for the door latch. Unlocked. I slammed my shoulder against it, but the weight of water slowed it to a weak shove. It didn't budge. I shoved again, and my elbow jabbed out the open window. Rolled down—I remembered it now. But only when I somersaulted out of my seat and my head hit the roof, did I understand I was upside down. I twisted and rolled, my entire brain consumed with finding an exit. *Air. I need air. Just one gulp.* Spots flickered and faded in front of my face like fireflies. *How long has it been? Thirty seconds? Get out! Get out now!*

As I pushed myself through the window, something hot stabbed into the underside of my arm. Glass, metal, I couldn't tell, only that it bit into my skin like teeth, the sting clearing my brain for a second. *Up! Go up!* I flipped over again and pulled my head around, forcing myself to keep my eyes open. Light above me. A round golden blob, flickering down on me through the water, shiny as a brass ball. The sun. The surface. My fingers clawed through weeds and grit and muck like an animal escaping a trap.

I pushed off as the last stream of bubbles flew from my mouth, pulling hard strokes, hand over hand, shedding my flip-flops with each kick, and in four strokes I broke the surface. The blue-and-gold light blinded my burning eyes, and my mouth flew open to scream. But the only sound I heard was the howling gasp of relief I made as air rushed in.

Immediately a voice cut through my panting heaves. "I got you! I got you!" Strong hands pulled my shoulders back.

"No!" I lurched away, spluttering. "Stop!"

"It's okay! You're gonna be okay."

"No! More!"

"You're in shock!" The hands clamped down tighter, swirling the water around me into a dark whirlpool; I was too shaky to fight.

"More people!" I screeched, bending my head down in a weak attempt to bite his hand.

"In the car?" The grip relaxed slightly. "I didn't see anyone!"

"Backseat!" I kicked out, elbowing his chest, using his torso as a wall to shove off. "One more person!"

Down I dove, my eyes strained open in the murk. Everything was shadows, dark gray-and-green blobs. Then below, a darker hulk, but I only realized it was the car when my fist punched the tire. *Where is she?* My ears popped when I swallowed, my fingers ran over the underside of the fender. *Is this the back? Where is the back?*

I pushed through an open window and banged my face against the headrest, my hands finding nothing. Empty. But when I grabbed again, thin feathery wisps brushed against my arms. Tendrils like seaweed. Hair. *She's here.* My head throbbed dully as my fingers worked up the length of the seat belt—the click of the button like a gunshot in my ears. I pulled her from the belt, but her arms were already cold and soft, pieces of soggy dough that might come apart in my hands. I jerked her forward, hard as I could, screaming into the water.

A silver ceiling. Hanging tubes and cords and rows of knobs and buttons. Blinking red and yellow lights. I swung my head around; my eyes rolled the opposite direction, spinning like forgotten marbles. Above my face, in front of white lights, someone said something to another person, a command or question, words that sounded like *Over here. Look at me. You're going to be all right. What is the ETA?* Were they talking to me? I couldn't answer. I didn't even care. I blinked and faded back to darkness.

A low buzz woke me. A hum—a repetitive mechanical beep keeping time with my heart. A cold hand gripped mine, then squeezed tightly as I blinked my eyes open. My mother's powdery perfume, dusty with the scent of lilies and roses, floated over me, and I lifted my head to ask the only thing I still didn't know. The plastic oxygen mask muffled my voice, but my mother knew what I asked. It was only a word. One question.

Under the fluorescent lights her eyes shimmered like rain-soaked pavement, but she didn't speak. She didn't say a word. She only bent her head forward and turned it, hiding her face away from mine.

Then I knew the answer.

Day 1
Late Morning

"Are you sure, Em? You don't have to go if you don't think you're ready."

"Christine, we've already discussed this. . . ."

"It's fine, Mom. We're already here," I said from the back-seat, watching the campers unload their gear in the gravel parking lot. They all seemed healthy. Strong and tan. Farm kids? City kids? The kind of kids whose moms probably had milk and cookies waiting for them after their varsity tennis meets or swim club. I focused on the back of one boy, lanky, shaggy hair, wearing a bright turquoise T-shirt and lugging a well-stuffed backpack over one shoulder. It was one of those serious models with a lightweight aluminum cage, water-proof ripstop nylon, and a million different hidey-holes. I had the same one.

I pressed my head against the window. "Besides, you've already paid for it."

"Honey, that's not important. If you don't feel up to it . . ."

"I know, Mom. But Dr. Nguyen thinks it will be a good thing. So do I," I tacked on at the end. *What I feel is irrelevant. It doesn't matter. It doesn't change anything.*

"Okay. Well, I'm just saying . . ." My mom stopped. Her voice was thin, stretched tight like a layer of ice over water. It wouldn't take much to break it. But I couldn't stand to see her start crying. Not again. Not here. You'd think a person would get to a point where they had nothing left. Like a well of water. Eventually you have to run dry, don't you?

"It's only a week," I reminded her. "And when I get back, I'll look into some of those college applications, okay?" There. That should convince her. It convinced my dad. I watched his shoulders sink behind the backrest, as if he was an inflatable device someone just stuck with a pin.

"That's good to hear, Emma," he said. "You could sign up for a few community college courses. Transfer in next semester."

I put my hand on the door latch. "That's the plan," I lied, knowing the deadline had already passed for the local community college fall semester. Over the past year my lies were coming faster and easier, sliding out of my mouth like spit. "It's cheaper to take the prereqs there, anyway." My dad smiled and nodded at the rearview mirror as he opened his door, satisfied.

I got out too; I didn't want my mom to see my face. My dad was easy to convince. He *wanted* to be convinced. He didn't look too far below the surface of things—I used to think it was because he didn't believe anything was there, but now I know better. Some people just don't want to turn over the rock and see the worms.

I stepped into the hot sun and stretched my arms over my head. Despite the heat, there was a smell in the air that reminded me of the inside of a freezer. The north woods had its own scent, and after a five-hour drive north we'd gone just about as far as you can go without crossing the Canadian border. Ely, Minnesota, to be exact. Population 3,471. Give or take. The gateway to the Boundary Waters Canoe Area, or BWCA, as the locals say. Last dot on the map before the wilderness.

My dad handed me my backpack with a smile. I don't know why he bought something like this; I never camp. Correction: We (the Dodd family) never camp. Have never camped. The closest we got was when I was ten and we stayed in a cabin at Jellystone Park.

But this whole thing had been my idea. I saw the BWCA brochure while I was waiting my turn in the counselor's office. I suppose I could have done homework, but that would have been a responsible use of my time. Instead I went through the stack of pamphlets on the table next to my chair, or, as I called them, illustrated cautionary tales. STDs. Smoking. Drugs. Drunk driving. The entire "don't do it or you'll be sorry" catalog, fanned out for my perusal.

I shuffled them like a deck of playing cards, until a flyer on the wall caught my eye. It was bright yellow, with a large outline of a bird on the top. A loon, I think. I could barely read the words, so I got up and walked over and ignored the sideways glance the receptionist gave me.

DO YOU HAVE WHAT IT TAKES?
Probably not.

HAVE YOU ALWAYS WANTED TO TEST YOUR LIMITS IN THE GREAT OUTDOORS?
Not especially.

LEARN TO LIVE OFF THE LAND BY YOUR WITS?
Shit, no. Most of those pioneers died of dysentery. I like my indoor plumbing, thanks.

BE A LEADER IN LIFE?
Uh, I'm a pretty good follower.

THEN JOIN US FOR A WEEK THAT WILL CHANGE YOUR LIFE!
Really? Only a week?

I stopped reading right there and ripped the flyer off the wall. I suppose I just could have written the information down and looked it up later, but some part of me knew that if I left the office without it, it would just be one more thing I failed to follow through on. I needed to steal it. Thankfully, the receptionist was too busy on the phone to notice.

That night I typed the website address into the computer.

It looked to be a non-Jesusy vacation adventure in the Boundary Waters. Very Boy Scouty. Very Outward Boundish. It was for teenagers at least fifteen. I stared at the pictures of perfect forest landscapes, fiery pink-and-orange sunsets, an owl perched up in a pine tree, people paddling canoes over lakes that looked like mirrors. There, I thought. I needed to go there. I hovered the cursor over the reservation tab, already knowing the conversation I would have with my parents. What I would say. What they would say. How I already knew this was a good idea. It was a forgone conclusion, as they say. A done deal. I clicked the button.

But that had been back in the beginning of April, when there were still dirty scabs of snow on the ground. Summer seemed impossible. Now it was the second week of August, and I stood blinking stupidly in the sun, wondering where I had put my sunglasses, while my dad unloaded all the gear from the back, smiling like it was Everest base camp and he was my own personal porter.

"Got everything?" My mom climbed out of the passenger seat.

"Yep." I didn't have a lot. Tents were provided, as were our meals. According to the website, campers were responsible for bringing a sleeping bag, hiking boots, a canteen, flashlight, warm jacket, gloves, sweatshirt, sweats, quick-dry hiking pants, personal toiletries, socks, sandals, swimsuit, sunblock, a hat, and of course (and probably most importantly) bug spray.

"Enough Off?"

"Two cans," I said. "With extra deet." I slung my new backpack over my shoulders and buckled the straps across my waist and chest. Despite being stuffed to the gills, the thing didn't feel very heavy. "I've got everything I need."

"Almost." My dad pressed something cold and smooth into my palm. "Take this."

I opened my hand to see a faded red Swiss Army knife. *A knife?* I swallowed and looked at my feet.

"David." My mom's voice wavered.

"I don't need this," I blurted. "Really, it's okay. It's not like we're going to have to hunt a moose or something."

My dad laughed. "You'd need more than that for a moose." My dad had hunted growing up. Hunted, fished, camped. But he was the only one in our family who enjoyed such things. My mom had always been more of a four-star-hotel type of person. Eggs benedict and bacon (extra crispy) for breakfast.

"And," my dad continued, "You probably won't need it. But you never know. . . ." He trailed off, looking over my head and refusing to acknowledge my mom's ashen face. The past year had been bad between them—I was the only one in the family seeing a shrink, but I certainly wasn't the only one who needed it. *I wonder if they'll get divorced.* In some ways it already seemed inevitable.

Yes, they definitely needed professional help. *Professional help.* I personally preferred the term "headshrinker." I always imagined some voodoo priest in face paint, his shaman stick dangling with a bunch of tiny shrunken heads.

I wonder what Dr. Nguyen would say if I told her that. Maybe want to give me medication. Then again, maybe not. I wasn't crazy, technically. And I wasn't suicidal, not really. I had bad thoughts. Dark thoughts. Horrible nightmares. Dr. Nguyen called it PTSD—post-traumatic stress disorder. Her words, not mine. Apparently I now had a disorder I thought was reserved only for soldiers who'd been in combat.

So the fact that my father was giving me a weapon and sending me off into the wilderness with total strangers made me think two things simultaneously:

My dad really trusts me.

My dad is crazier than I am.

"Thanks, Dad." I didn't open the blades but tucked it quickly into the back pocket of my jeans. "I know it was Grandpa's. I'll make sure to take good care of it."

"From the war." My dad nodded. "He said it was lucky. He said it saved his life."

"Okay." I didn't know what else to say to that.

My parents hugged me hard, too tight and too long, but I let them, barely flinching when my mom kissed my cheek.

"I love you, Emma."

"Me too." It was all I could manage. I couldn't bring myself to say the words even if I felt them. "See you next week." I shrugged out of their arms and turned toward the far side of the lot, to where a pack of kids had gathered in front of an older man with a salt-and-pepper beard, faded Twins ball cap, and mirrored aviator shades. He stood under a hand-painted sign (INTO THE WOODS) and held a clipboard. There was a shiny silver whistle around his neck, so I guessed he was in charge. That's all you needed to look official. Sunglasses, clipboard, whistle. He could be a serial killer for all we knew.

I crunched across the hot gravel in my new hiking boots, following a tall, athletic-looking girl with a red bandana tied around her forehead. *She's probably done this before.*

I was in decent shape, physically speaking, but I had never portaged a canoe. This girl had strong-looking shoulders, with well-defined arm muscles—she could probably portage canoes in her sleep.

"Welcome, everyone!" The bearded man waved us closer. "This is going to be some trip! The day's a-wasting, so hustle up!"

Hustle up? He sounded like my JV basketball coach.

"My name's Chris, and I'll be your team leader and guide. Are you guys ready for the week of your life?"

Crickets. I looked around. Four boys, two girls, including myself. *This is it?*

"Um," said the tall girl, saying what everyone else was probably thinking. "Where's everyone else?"

"We can take up to nine," Chris explained. "But there were a couple cancellations."

"Great," said the girl, almost to herself. She turned around and winked at me, probably as relieved as I was that there was at least one other female. "Looks like a total sausage fest," she whispered, but loud enough for everyone to hear.

I liked her immediately.

Chris scanned the sheet on the board. "Are you Emma or Chloe?"

"Chloe Johnson," replied the girl smoothly, not missing a beat. She stepped back so we were standing next to each other. "This here is my sister, Emma."

Chris looked up, then down, then back up at me. "Emma Dodd?"

"That's me," I said, instantly hating how unconfident I sounded, as if I was apologizing for being there.

"All right," said Chris. "Where is Isaac Bergstrom?"

"Here." A tall blond boy sitting on the picnic table answered.

"Jeremy Vernon?"

"Yep."

"Wes Villarreal?"

"Here."

Wes and Jeremy stood side by side, obviously friends. They had probably decided to sign up together, which was a smart idea. Once again it hadn't occurred to me to ask one of my friends, though my friends had been in short supply the past year. Only Shelly still called me to hang out, though I usually never did. Most everyone else avoided me, socially speaking. Can't say that I blamed them.

"Oscar O'Brien?"

"That's me." It was the boy in the turquoise T-shirt. He pushed his glasses back up the bridge of his nose.

"Great, looks like we're all here. Let's go." Chris turned and started walking, and we all stood there momentarily, as if the whole idea was just a joke. Isaac slid off the table and followed; the rest of us did the same.

"We're going to the outfitters," Chris explained as he walked us to a large white conversion van. *Serial-killer van.* "We'll pick up our food and supplies, sign in, and go through a safety check." He opened a van door and motioned us forward. "Time's a-wasting! We got a lot of ground to cover in a week. Literally."

The sun disappeared behind a thick cloud, and an icy breeze gusted down over the treetops, making me shiver through my sweat. A warning? I think in the movies they called that foreshadowing.

This is probably a bad idea. I couldn't help the thought; it made me turn around and look for my parent's dark gray Subaru. But they had already gone.